Charlie Lupton and the Ultimate Challenge

Also by Nigel A. Bernard:

Charlie Lupton's Sherpa Adventure
Charlie Lupton and the Cavalier's Treasure
Charlie Lupton and the Orchid Princess
Charlie Lupton and the Secret Satellite
Charlie Lupton and the Hi-Tech Kid

The Osprey Enigma

Charlie Lupton and the Ultimate Challenge

Nigel A. Bernard

First published in Great Britain in 2022
by Okay Let's Read
Pembroke Dock
okayletsread@outlook.com

www.nigelbernard.com

Facebook: Charlie Lupton Adventures

Copyright © 2022 Nigel A. Bernard

All rights reserved; no part of this publication may be reproduced or transmitted by any means, electronic, mechanical, photocopying or otherwise, without the prior permission of the publisher.

ISBN 978-1-4709-9682-6

This is a work of fiction. Any resemblance to actual people, living or dead, is entirely coincidental.

1	The overhang	1
2	Stand back	11
3	Handling history	21
4	Dewhurst the dietician	32
5	Auntie Edith explains	43
6	The climbing wall	53
7	Searching for thruppence	62
8	Lightbulb moment	73
9	The garden secret	83
10	The garden plan	94
11	The garden challenge	105
12	With a little help	116
13	The dyno	127
14	Beyond the rooftops	138

– CHAPTER 1 –

The overhang

Charlie Lupton was scared. Maybe it would be wiser not to go in. It is better to be safe than sorry. But the gate was unlocked. Why not go in? He craned his neck and looked up. The fence was many times higher than he was. If the way back to the gate was blocked there was no way he could climb the fence.

He bit his lip and told himself there was nothing to worry about. Surely it would be safe? But that's not what the big sign said. He read it one more time.

Danger – Lions Can Kill.

He took a deep breath and walked in.

If the others in his class were nervous, they didn't show it.

'This is randomly epic,' said Mickey Dewhurst, as he took a photo of the enclosure on his phone. 'I don't usually like Mondays at school, but this is exciting.'

'You don't like any days at school,' said Geraldine Primrose.

'That's true,' said Mickey. 'For once you and I agree on something. We both agree I don't like school on any day.'

'Come on, quickly everybody,' said Mrs Drake, as the rest of the class walked in. 'We mustn't take up too much of Mr Ely's time.'

'There's no rush,' said Mr Ely as he held up his hands. 'Now, folks, gather round and I'll tell you all about this enclosure.'

Then Penny Elliot put up her hand.

'Yes, young lady,' said Mr Ely.

'Are ... are there really no lions in here?'

This made Charlie feel better. He wasn't the only one feeling nervous after all.

'No, I can assure you there are no lions in here,' said Mr Ely, laughing. 'The lions will be arriving later this week. As the newly appointed head lion keeper at the park, I am really looking forward to giving them a nice new home. As you can see, it's a very large enclosure. And it's very secure. The big gate you all walked through will be permanently locked before the lions arrive. The fence is made of steel and is fourteen feet high. And there is a three-and-a-half-foot overhang at the top.'

Charlie looked at the top of the fence and saw the way the fence was bent inwards. He knew about overhangs. Some rock-climbing routes have overhangs.

'Even if the lions could climb that high,' said Mr Ely, 'they would never get over the overhang.'

'Could you climb that?' somebody whispered to Charlie.

He turned round. It was Emma Appleyard.

'I'm not sure,' said Charlie. 'I've never tried to climb an overhang. They're tricky.'

Other children started to chatter too.

'Quiet everybody,' said Mrs Drake.

'Let me tell you a little about the enclosure,' said Mr Ely. 'That small gate over there leads into the yard. Beyond that, gated tunnels lead to the rooms where the lions can sleep.

When they arrive we will put them straight in there and only let them out for the first time once they've settled.'

Geraldine put her hand up.

'Yes, young lady,' said Mr Ely.

'Those rooms and the yard look very small. Isn't it really just a like a zoo?'

'No, they will spend most of their time outside here in the enclosure itself,' said Mr Ely. 'As you can see, it's very big, around seven acres in fact. There is plenty of room for the lions to roam. And it's got features which make it interesting for the lions like trees, a small lake and a couple of large mounds. Oh, and we've got that old Land Rover over there painted with black and white stripes like a zebra, just like the ones driven in the plains of Africa by game wardens.'

'That is awesome,' said Mickey, as he took a photo of the Land Rover.

'Now, let me tell you about the lions that are coming later this week,' said Mr Ely. 'It is a pride of six lions coming from South Downs Safari Park. There is Mason, the king of the pride. He is six years old. Then there is Amelia the lioness, she is five years old. And coming with Mason and Amelia will be their four cubs, which are nine months old. They will be arriving on Thursday. So if you see a large lorry driving through Heatherbridge on Thursday afternoon with South Downs Safari Park written on the side you had better watch out. It will be full of lions!'

Everybody started murmuring.

'Now,' said Mr Ely, 'you can have a couple of minutes to wander around the enclosure. Then I'm afraid I will have to leave you as I have a meeting to attend. I hope you are enjoying your visit to Heatherbridge Wildlife Park.'

'We certainly are enjoying our visit,' said Mrs Drake. 'Thank you very much for your time. It is not everybody who can say they have been inside a lion's enclosure! Now children, have a quick wander around then we can go down to the picnic benches and eat our packed lunches.'

'Let's go to the top of that mound,' said Emma. 'We'll get a better view.'

'That's a good idea,' said Geraldine.

'You two coming?' said Emma.

'I guess so,' said Charlie.

'I'm going to have a look at the Land Rover,' said Mickey. He walked off with his hands in his pockets.

Charlie, Emma and Geraldine trudged up the mound and finally got to the top and sat on some rocks.

'Just think,' said Emma, 'this is where Mason the king of the pride will sit.'

'I still don't think the enclosure is really big enough,' said Geraldine. 'I'm sure he and his pride would prefer to be roaming free in Africa.'

'They will be fine,' said Emma. 'They will be looked after and well fed.'

Charlie looked around, taking in the view. At this height they were nearly level with the top of the fence away in the distance. Charlie studied the way it was bent inwards, almost at right angles to the vertical part of the fence. He wondered what it must be like to climb an overhang.

'Come on everybody, it's time to go.'

They looked down the mound to see Miss Rees, the classroom assistant, calling them. They got up and walked with the rest of the class to the gate. As Charlie went out he felt a sense of relief. He looked up again at the warning message and he felt a shiver go down his spine.

'Well, that will be something to tell your mums and dads when you get home,' said Mr Ely as he slammed the gate shut and locked it. 'You can all tell them Mrs Drake let you go inside the lion enclosure!'

Everybody laughed.

'I've got to go now,' he said. 'Cheerio everybody.'

Everybody said 'goodbye' as he walked off.

'Now children,' said Mrs Drake, 'please walk quietly down to the picnic benches. Please be mindful of other visitors in the park. There is also a class from another school visiting so let's show them we know how to behave.'

They walked down to the picnic benches. Their packed lunches had been stored in a room nearby and Miss Rees and a couple of volunteers from the class brought them over.

Charlie, Emma and Geraldine sat at one of the benches. Penny was nearby looking unsure where to sit.

'Come and sit with us,' said Emma.

'Thanks,' she said.

They began eating their lunch.

'Where's Mickey?' said Emma.

'I dunno,' said Charlie. 'He's probably over there with the twins.'

'Well, I'm not complaining,' said Geraldine. 'It's nice to have a quiet civilized lunch for a change. We should be grateful to Darren and Jonny for sharing the burden.'

'That's not very nice,' said Emma. 'Anyway, I don't think he is with the twins. I can't see him over there.'

'Has everybody got their lunch?' shouted Miss Rees. 'I've got one left over.'

Nobody said anything and kept on eating.

After a little while they heard what sounded like laughing and shouting.

'It's that class from the other school,' said Geraldine. 'I'm so glad I don't go to that school.'

'But why are they all looking into the lion enclosure?' said Emma. 'There's nothing to see.'

'Perhaps the lions have come early,' said Penny.

'Of course they haven't,' said Geraldine.

Charlie looked over to the enclosure. Other visitors in the park were also beginning to gather by the fence.

'What is going on over there?' said Mrs Drake as she stood up to have a better look.

'Uh, I think,' said Miss Rees, 'it might have something to do with this.' She had got up too and was holding the spare packed lunch.

'What do you mean?' said Mrs Drake.

Charlie looked at the packed lunch and then back across to the enclosure. Miss Rees, was right, he thought. It had everything to do with the spare packed lunch.

'Let's go and have a look,' said Emma. 'Perhaps some strange creature from another part of the park has got in.'

Charlie got up and as he did so, Miss Rees came over to him.

'You might like to take this,' she said.

'Thanks,' said Charlie, as he took the packed lunch off her.

'What did she mean?' said Emma as they started walking.

'Oh no,' said Geraldine. 'I know what's happened. I do not believe it. I think you're right, Emma. There is a strange creature in the lion enclosure. One of the strangest, weirdest creatures ever known to mankind.'

'How exciting,' said Emma, 'I must take a photo when I get there.'

'I don't think you will,' said Charlie. 'I don't think this creature is very photogenic.'

'What do you mean?' said Emma.

Then they reached the crowd. They stood on tiptoe to see what everyone was looking at. And there, standing inside the enclosure, was Mickey.

'Don't just stand there gawping,' he shouted. 'Get someone to unlock the gate!'

But everybody just laughed and kept taking pictures.

'He's bringing the name of Heatherbridge Junior School into disrepute,' said Geraldine.

They pushed their way to the front of the crowd.

'What are you doing in there?' shouted Charlie.

'I'm entertaining the visitors. What do you think I'm doing in here? I got locked in.'

'But how?' said Charlie.

'I was busy taking pictures of the Land Rover and got inside to see if I could take it for a spin. Next thing I know the place is deserted. Anyway, never mind that, get someone to unlock the gate.'

'But Mr Ely's got the keys and he's gone to a meeting,' said Emma.

'There must be someone else with a key,' said Mickey.

'This is SO embarrassing,' said Geraldine.

'Anyway, I'm getting hungry,' said Mickey, who was beginning to sound a bit upset.

'We can't feed him,' somebody from the other school said. 'There are signs everywhere saying, "don't feed the animals".'

Everybody started laughing again.

'Very funny,' said Mickey. He got down on the grass and sat cross-legged, looking very miserable.

'I've got your packed lunch here,' said Charlie.

'Well, what are you waiting for?' said Mickey, as he got up. 'Throw it over.'

'Okay,' said Charlie.

He took a few steps back as people made room for him. He threw it up as hard as he could. It went over the top of the fence, but then landed on the overhang.

'Oh, great,' said Mickey, as he looked up at his packed lunch. 'That's just brilliant. What am I supposed to do now?'

'It's a shame lions can't climb up fences,' said one of the onlookers.

'That's not a lion,' said somebody else. 'It looks more like a meerkat.'

'Very funny,' said Mickey.

By now the rest of the class had reached the fence.

'Mickey Dewhurst, what are you doing?' said Mrs Drake.

But Mickey just sat down and looked miserable.

Then a member of the park staff came up to them.

'I'm afraid, young lady, one of my pupils got left behind in the enclosure,' said Mrs Drake.

'That's no problem,' she said. 'Another member of staff with a key is nearby round the other side near the gate. I'll radio him to unlock it.'

She got on the radio and a few moments later there was the noise of the gate being opened.

'Look out mate!' somebody from the other school shouted. 'The lions have arrived early. They're letting them in.'

Mickey jumped up, ran to the Land Rover, got inside and slammed the door shut.

Meanwhile, everybody was laughing and taking more pictures.

'Unbelievable,' said Geraldine, shaking her head. 'Unbelievable'.

'That Mickey Dewhurst is a tinker,' said Mother, as Charlie finished telling his parents what had happened as they sat at dinner that evening.

'I don't blame him,' said Father. 'I've always fancied owning a Land Rover.'

'Really,' said Mother, as she got up and gathered the empty plates together. 'We're not having a Land Rover.'

'Well, perhaps I could paint the car with black and white stripes instead,' said Father as he winked at Charlie.

'Perhaps the both of you could help clear the table,' she said. She walked out with a sigh into the kitchen.

'Charlie, you haven't forgotten about the climbing competition?' said Father as they got up.

'No. It's not soon is it?'

'It's a week on Saturday,' said Father.

'Okay,' said Charlie.

'It will be a good experience for you. It will be just lead climbing and not bouldering. We'll be using the climbing wall at Heatherbridge High School. There should be quite a few climbers in your age group. It will be fun.'

'What is the climbing wall like at the school?' asked Charlie.

'Here, I'll show you,' said Father. He grabbed his laptop and brought up a photograph of the wall on the screen. 'You have to see how high you can get without falling off. Each climber is roped, of course, they're belayed by somebody at the bottom.'

'It looks okay,' said Charlie. 'I should be able to get to the top.'

Father laughed. 'Yes, well, I'm not so sure. You see this photograph is taken from the front. Here's a side view.'

Charlie looked and bit his lip.

'It's won't be easy, will it?' said Father.

Charlie scanned the wall from the bottom to the top. At first it seemed straight forward, but near the top there was a large overhang, maybe three times longer than the fence at the lion enclosure. Then the wall finished with a few vertical feet to the top. The overhang on the fence seemed bad enough, but the overhang on the climbing wall seemed impossible.

– CHAPTER 2 –

Stand back

'I still can't believe what happened yesterday,' said Geraldine. She was sitting on a log with Charlie and Emma in the natural play area waiting for the start of school.

'It wasn't his fault he got locked in,' said Emma.

'Of course it was his fault,' said Geraldine. 'He shouldn't have got in the Land Rover.'

'He was just being inquisitive,' said Emma. 'That's a sign of intelligence.'

'If it is, it's the first sign of intelligence he's ever shown,' said Geraldine.

'That's not very nice,' said Emma, 'I think you should be …'

Emma stopped speaking and they all looked towards the main gate. People in the school grounds were running and screaming. Some towards the school, others onto the field.

'What's happening?' asked Emma.

'I dunno,' said Charlie. 'Everybody sounds frightened.'

'Yes, but they are also laughing,' said Emma.

The way to the gate was now clear of children. Apart from one person, who had come through the gate and was walking over towards the natural play area.

'It's Mickey,' said Emma, 'Why are they all running away from him?'

Then a couple of children ran past them, waving their hands in the air, laughing and shouting. 'Look out! Look out! It's a lion!'

Mickey kept walking, looking fed up. There were children on either side, forming a gangway and pretending to be scared.

'Stand back,' somebody shouted, 'he might attack.'

Eventually, he reached the log and sat down. All the children then dispersed and carried on playing.

'I can't stand this,' said Mickey, as he sat with his arms folded.

'At least they didn't say you were a meerkat,' said Emma.

Mickey grunted.

'It's unbelievable,' said Geraldine. 'The whole incident was an embarrassment to our school.'

'Well, I thought overall the visit to the wildlife park went very well,' said Emma. 'Wouldn't you agree, Charlie?'

'Yes,' said Charlie. 'It was a roaring success.'

'Oh, that is hilarious,' said Mickey, sounding even more fed up.

Then the bell went and everybody walked into the school.

After assembly, they returned to the classroom.

'Please get to your tables and quieten down,' said Mrs Drake.

Charlie sat at the table with Mickey, Geraldine and Emma.

'Now, as you know,' said Mrs Drake, 'tomorrow morning we will be visiting the supermarket. You will have an activity sheet to complete while you are there. You will learn lots of facts about food. Each year I have taken previous classes and the visit is always informative.'

'I can't wait,' muttered Mickey.

'On all previous visits, we have made use of some excellent fruit and vegetable costumes which were made by an enterprising parent a few years ago. There are three vegetables and three fruits. So I would like six volunteers to wear these tomorrow at the supermarket. Their job will be to encourage customers to eat more fruit and vegetables. Please can I have six volunteers?'

A couple of people put their hands up but nobody seemed that keen.

'There must be more of you who would like to dress up,' said Mrs Drake.

'As a fruit or vegetable?' muttered Mickey. 'I don't think so.'

By now three more people had put their hand up.

'Well, if anybody else is interested in taking part, let me know,' said Mrs Drake. 'Now while the rest of us work on our multiplication exercise sheets, I would like the volunteers to go with Miss Rees to try on the costumes and make sure they fit.'

'Uh?' said Mickey. He put his hand up as high as it could go.

'Yes, Mickey,' said Mrs Drake.

'I would like to be a fruit or a vegetable, please.'

'Why the sudden enthusiasm?' said Mrs Drake.

'I like fruit and vegetables.'

'That's nonsense,' said Geraldine. 'You prefer crisps.'

'They're made from potatoes,' said Mickey, 'And last I heard, potatoes are vegetables.'

'This is ridiculous,' said Geraldine. 'He just wants to get out of doing maths.'

'Well, I'm sure Mickey's motives are honourable,' said Mrs Drake. But she didn't sound convinced. 'Now will our volunteers please go with Miss Rees and I will hand out the exercise sheets.'

Mickey gave a thumbs up, got up, and left the room with the other volunteers.

'At least we can get some work done now,' said Geraldine.

Everybody settled down and started working. Charlie reckoned the multiplication calculations were pretty difficult. Maybe Mickey had the right idea, he thought.

Charlie was working on a particularly difficult sum when the classroom door opened.

'Ah, the fruit and vegetable delivery has arrived,' said Mrs Drake.

Miss Rees had walked in and was holding the door. Then there was the strange sight of a carrot walking into the room. It was nearly as tall as the door. A girl's face could be seen poking through a circular hole in the material. She was followed by a pineapple, a strawberry, a peapod and a parsnip. They stood in front of the class with their faces poking through the holes in the costumes. Everybody else in the class were laughing and clapping.

Charlie looked at all the faces. There were three girls and two boys. But neither of the boys were Mickey.

Miss Rees was still holding the door open.

'I wonder what Mickey is,' said Emma.

'He'll be a potato,' said Geraldine. 'That's if he's been true to his roots.'

Charlie looked at Geraldine. She looked quite pleased with her joke.

But then there was a bang and a grunt coming from just outside the door. 'I can hardly see where I'm going,' shouted a muffled voice.

Miss Rees stretched out her hand into the corridor. 'This way,' she said. 'More to your left.' She then stood back as Mickey walked in.

'That's not a potato,' said Emma. 'That's an orange'.

Everybody looked at the strange sight of a large spherical orange with two spindly legs and two spindly arms sticking out. The orange itself looked like it was made from papier-mâché. There was no big gap in the front for a face. There were just two small holes to look through.

'Hey, Mickey,' somebody shouted, 'what's the time?'

The left arm of the orange lifted up but of course, Mickey couldn't see his arm, let alone his watch.

The words 'very funny,' were heard from inside the orange, as the arm went back down.

'I presume that is Mickey Dewhurst inside that orange,' said Mrs Drake.

Miss Rees lifted the top half of the sphere off to reveal Mickey's head. He didn't look very happy.

'Well, I'm glad the costumes are still usable,' said Mrs Drake. 'You all look very realistic and I am sure the customers will be encouraged to eat more fruit and vegetables. Now please go back to the music room and get out of your costumes. You will then have to work extra hard on your sums to catch up.'

'I don't mind staying like this,' said Mickey. 'It will get me used to wearing ...' But at this point Miss Rees plonked the top half of the orange back over Mickey's head. All that could be heard now were muffled sounds. Everybody laughed as the protesting Mickey was turned around by Miss Rees and pointed in the general direction of the doorway.

After they had eaten lunch Charlie and Mickey went out onto the field. A group of boys were setting up goals with their sweatshirts.

'Mickey, are you going to play football?' somebody shouted.

'He prefers rugby,' somebody else said. 'He wants to play for the British and Irish Lions.'

'Very funny,' said Mickey. 'Come on mate, let's go and sit in the shade. It's too hot for football.'

They sat down on a log in the natural play area.

'What was it like in that orange?' asked Charlie.

'It's a nightmare. It's hot and dark. Still, at least I can't be seen. Nobody will know it's me. I can just stand quiet and no one will bother me. No one's going to want to be seen talking to an orange.'

'But you're supposed to encourage people to eat fruit and vegetables.'

'It'll be impossible in that thing. Anyway, the other good thing is that I won't have to do the activity sheet.'

'Have you got room for us on the log?' It was Emma, and she had Geraldine with her.

'It might be a squash, Emma,' said Geraldine. 'But Mickey won't mind. After all, he is an orange.'

'That's pathetic,' said Mickey. 'Anyway, I didn't know you had a sense of humour.'

'Geraldine cracked another funny joke this morning,' said Emma. 'It was about roots.'

'The only route I'm interested in is the route out of here,' said Mickey.

'That route is spelt with a *u*,' said Geraldine.

'Ah, that's a relief,' said Mickey. 'The old Geraldine has returned.'

'What's all that digging over there?' asked Emma.

On the edge of the play area, there was a large rectangular patch of freshly dug earth where the grass had been. It was about the size of a car parking space.

'I saw the caretaker digging it this morning,' said Charlie.

'It's for the Year Fives,' said Geraldine. 'I heard some of them talking about it. They're going to plant some autumn crocuses.'

'It's a bit late for planting isn't it?' said Emma. 'It's the middle of summer.'

'These will grow over summer and flower next term,' said Geraldine. 'That's why they're called autumn crocuses.'

Charlie turned to look at Mickey. He was staring at the patch of ground. 'It's just a patch of soil, Mickey,' he said.

Mickey grunted. 'There's something there,' he said. He stood up and walked over to it. He bent down and was looking at a spot on the edge near the grass. He then got up, went into the undergrowth of the natural play area, found a thick twig lying on the ground and walked back to the same spot.

'Mickey, what are you doing?' asked Geraldine.

They watched as he started scraping at something with the twig. It was a sort of brown-coloured metal and looked like the bottom of a tin.

By now they had all got up to have a look.

'It's just the bottom of an old tin of soup or something,' said Geraldine.

'It looks like it might be longer than that,' said Emma. 'It looks like it goes well under the grass'

'Why don't you just pull it out?' said Charlie. He bent down to grab hold of it.

'I wouldn't do that if I was you,' said Mickey. 'This isn't just an old soup tin.'

'What is it then?' asked Emma.

Mickey looked down at it and then looked at each of them in turn. 'It's obvious what it is. It's an unexploded wartime bomb.'

'What?' said Emma. 'A bomb? Are you sure?'

'I know all about this kind of thing,' said Mickey. 'I'm a military expert.'

'You're not a military expert,' said Geraldine. 'I don't think it's a bomb.'

'Well, go ahead and pull it out,' said Mickey.

But Geraldine didn't seem keen.

'What's going on?' said one of the boys who had been playing football and had come over to look.

'Stand back,' said Mickey. 'It's a bomb,'.

'Hey everybody,' shouted the boy to the others playing football. 'Come and look at this. It's a bomb.'

With that, they all ran over. In no time what seemed like most of the school had gathered round.

'Stand back, stand back,' said Mickey.

Then a teacher who was on lunch duty came over.

'What's going on?' she said.

'Mickey's found a bomb,' somebody said.

'Let me have a look,' she said.

They let her through and she looked down at the object in the ground.

'Is it a bomb?' somebody asked.

Charlie thought the teacher seemed a bit worried. But then she looked back toward the school. 'It looks like Mr Metcalfe is coming over,' said the teacher, sounding relieved.

They all turned to look. Sure enough, Mr Metcalfe, the head teacher, was striding across the grass.

'What is going on here?' he asked.

'The children have found something in the soil,' said the teacher.

'Who found it?' asked Mr Metcalfe, as he looked down it.

'I did,' said Mickey. 'I told everybody it was a bomb and to stand back. But they wouldn't listen.'

'Mickey if this is a bomb there's no point in people just standing back is there?' said Mr Metcalfe.

'You're right,' said Mickey. 'Okay, everybody. You heard what Mr Metcalfe said. We need to get as far away as we can. Everybody go home.'

With that, everybody started to go away. Some were cheering.

'Everybody just calm down,' said Mr Metcalfe. 'I said nothing about going home, or even moving back.'

'Is it really a bomb, Mr Metcalfe?' asked Emma.

'Of course, it is,' said Mickey.

'Mickey, what makes you so sure?' said Mr Metcalfe.

'He told us he was a military expert,' said Geraldine. 'He must be right.' She huffed and shook her head.

Mr Metcalfe bent down and pulled the object out a couple of inches. As he did so some children gasped and sounded worried. 'I thought so, I thought so,' said Mr Metcalfe as he looked at the object. 'Mickey, I would agree that this may well be from the Second World War era.'

Mickey turned to Charlie and gave him a thumbs up.

'Now, Mickey, I have a question for you. Drawing on your knowledge as a military expert, exactly what kind of weapon do you think the company Dunlop was making at that time?'

'Uh?' said Mickey.

'That's the name on this suspected bomb,' said Mr Metcalfe, pointing at the words on its side. 'Well, any ideas, Mickey?'

'Uh, well, maybe it's not a bomb,' said Mickey. 'Maybe they just made small things, like hand grenades.'

'Hand grenades?' said Mr Metcalfe. 'Well, I've got another suggestion. How about tennis balls?' He pulled hard on the object and it came out of the ground. It was a tin tube about nine inches long. It had a label with a picture of tennis balls.

Everybody started laughing and sounding very relieved.

'Well, that's your bomb, Mickey,' said Mr Metcalfe. He handed it to Mickey.

Mickey stood examining it, looking a bit sheepish. Then he gave it a shake. There was the sound of loose objects rattling inside. 'That doesn't sound like tennis balls,' said Mickey.

'Look,' said Geraldine. 'There's some handwriting on the label.' She took it off Mickey and read it out loud. 'Time Capsule. September 2nd 1945. Edith Emma Elliot. Aged 10.'

'What's a time capsule when it's at home?' asked Mickey.

'It's when somebody puts important items in a container to be opened by a future generation,' said Geraldine. 'I wonder what's inside it.'

'Well,' said Mr Metcalfe, 'there's only one way to find out.'

– CHAPTER 3 –

Handling history

'Right,' said Mr Metcalfe, 'what will be the best way to do this?'

He had taken the time capsule off Geraldine and was still standing by the patch of soil where it had been found.

'Can we open it now, Mr Metcalfe?' said Geraldine. 'It is so exciting.'

'Yes, it is exciting,' said Mr Metcalfe. 'But we certainly don't want to be opening it out here. We might lose something if there are small items. Also, the top of the tin seems to be jammed on tight. It might need to be prised open.'

Dozens of children were gathered around looking expectantly at Mr Metcalfe.

'I think,' said Mr Metcalfe, 'as Mickey was the one that found it we should let his class be the first to find out what's inside. I will take it to Mrs Drake in the staffroom and explain what has happened. I have to go into town to a meeting this afternoon. I will be interested to know what you find inside. Right, carry on, everybody.'

Everybody moved away and Mr Metcalfe walked off towards the school.

'It is so exciting,' said Geraldine. 'I can't wait for it to be opened.'

'It's going to be gripping,' said Mickey. 'I don't think I can stand the suspense.'

After lunch break, they all returned to the classroom. When they walked in the time capsule was on the table at the front. Some children stopped to look at it.

'Everybody sit down to begin with,' said Mrs Drake. 'There will be plenty of opportunity to examine it this afternoon. Miss Rees and myself have decided to abandon the craft session we planned for this lesson. We will do some history instead.'

'This afternoon is going from bad to worse,' said Mickey as he sat down by Charlie. 'First I mistake a tin of tennis balls for a bomb, now I'm stuck in a history lesson.'

'Before we open the capsule,' said Mrs Drake, 'we need to try and work out some facts from what is written on the tin. We know that a ten-year-old girl made and apparently buried the time capsule on 2 September 1945. Does anybody know the significance of that date?'

A girl near the back put her hand up.

'Yes, Claire,' said Mrs Drake.

'Perhaps it was her birthday.'

'It might have been,' said Mrs Drake. 'But I wonder if this date is important in history. Has anybody else got any ideas? Yes, Darren.'

'Is it something to do with the war?'

'Excellent, I think it might well be,' said Mrs Drake. 'But which war do you mean?'

'The Second World War,' said Darren.

'Well done, Darren. Can anybody tell us some facts about the Second World War? Mickey, you found the capsule. Do you know any facts about the war?'

Mickey thought for a moment then his face lit up. 'Britain won it in 1940. They won the Battle of Britain.'

'Well, they didn't win the war in that year,' said Mrs Drake. 'But Britain did win the Battle of Britain. Where was the battle fought?'

'In the air,' said Mickey. 'It was between the British air force and the German air force.'

'Excellent, Mickey,' said Mrs Drake.

'I told you I was a military expert,' muttered Mickey.

'Except you can't tell the difference between a bomb and a tin of tennis balls,' said Geraldine.

'Anyway, it might be explosives,' said Mickey. 'Whatever's inside it, it's not tennis balls.'

'Now, we've established that the Battle of Britain was fought in 1940,' said Mrs Drake. 'But does anybody know when the Second World War started?'

Geraldine put her hand up.

'Yes, Geraldine.'

'1939, when Germany invaded Poland.'

'That's correct,' said Mrs Drake. 'Germany invaded Poland on 1 September 1939. Britain declared war on Germany two days later on 3 September.'

'Does anybody know what happened after that?' asked Mrs Drake.

Nobody put their hand up.

'It's a bit of a trick question,' said Mrs Drake. 'To start with, except for what was going on in Poland, nothing much happened elsewhere. Some people called it the 'phoney war' because there wasn't much fighting, certainly not by the British. But all that changed in May 1940 when Germany invaded France. There were some British forces in France and they had to flee to the coast. Does anybody know the name of the French town on the coast where the British forces gathered on the beach?'

Darren put his hand up.

'Yes, Darren.'

'Was it Dunkirk?'

'Well, done, Darren,' said Mrs Drake. 'Yes, the British soldiers gathered on the beach at Dunkirk. Thousands were rescued by small boats from England. People volunteered to take their boats across the channel and rescue them. They were very brave because enemy planes were bombing the beaches. But all this was way before our date on the time capsule. So, are there any more ideas about the importance of 2 September 1945?'

Geraldine put her had up.

'Yes, Geraldine.'

'Was that the day the Second World War ended?'

'Well done, Geraldine. Yes, the war officially ended that day. That was the day the Japanese formally signed the surrender document. Peace had already come to Europe. Germany had surrendered four months earlier in May.'

Everybody stayed quiet for a moment.

'It was a long war, wasn't it?' said Emma.

'It was Emma,' said Mrs Drake. 'It might sound exciting but it wasn't like that. Many people suffered and many people lost their lives. Now, to the matter in hand. Does anybody know when our school was built?'

'1962,' said Geraldine.

'That's correct,' said Mrs Drake. 'Before that time the area where the school is now was just meadows and a few trees. It was a good place for children to come and play. And it was evidently a good place to bury a time capsule. Now the exciting moment has arrived when the time capsule will be opened. Please will everybody now calmly gather round this table.'

Everybody got up and walked to the front.

'Miss Rees,' said Mrs Drake, 'perhaps you would like to have the honour of opening it.'

Miss Rees tried to take the lid off. 'It won't budge,' she said.

'We don't want you breaking a nail,' said Mrs Drake. 'Here, prise it off with this,' she said, as she took a screwdriver out of a drawer.

Miss Rees placed the tip of the screwdriver under the lid and then forced the screwdriver downwards as she tried to lever the lid off. At first, nothing happened, but then the lid moved a fraction. She moved the screwdriver further round to another part of the lid. The lid came up a little more. By now there was a clear gap between the lid and the tin. Miss Rees put the screwdriver an inch inside the tin and gave one final push on the handle. She then put the screwdriver down and pulled the lid with her fingers. There was a puff of dust and the lid came off.

Miss Rees placed the lid on the table and looked into the tin. 'There are a few cobwebs,' she said.

'I think the best thing is to tip it upside down and see what comes out,' said Mrs Drake. 'Mickey, as you found it I think you should do that. Come round to the front here so everybody can see.'

Mickey walked round to the front. He picked up the tin and looked inside.

'Careful, Mickey,' a boy said. 'It might be packed with explosive.'

Everybody laughed.

'Very funny,' said Mickey, who then sneezed as dust from the tin drifted upwards. He wafted the dust away and then began to turn the tin upside down. There was the sound of rolling and four colourful marbles bounced onto the table. Mickey turned the tin upright again and managed to grab the marbles before they rolled off.

'Put them on the lid so they won't roll any further,' said Mrs Drake.

After he had put them on the upturned lid he once more started turning the tin upside down. The next thing to drop out was a jagged piece of metal. Mickey picked it up and looked at it.

'That's pretty boring,' he said, and put it to one side.

'Mickey just turn the tin completely upside down close to the table,' said Mrs Drake.

With that, the rest of the contents of the tin emptied onto the table.

'Excellent,' said Mickey, as two toy cars fell out, 'Dinky cars. This is a Sportsman Coupe,' he said, as he held one of the cars up and it turned it round, examining it.

'How do you know?' asked Geraldine. 'Are you a car expert as well?'

'You can tell by its shape,' said Mickey, sounding like an expert. 'You can also tell by the fact that it's got the words "Sportsman Coupe" written underneath.' He grinned at Geraldine and put it down on the table.

Geraldine huffed.

'And this is not a car, it's actually a tram,' he said, as he pointed to the other Dinky toy.

'What is that brown tag?' said Emma.

Mrs Drake picked it up. It was about the size of a playing card and one end was pointed with a piece of brown string tied through a hole. 'It has the words "London County Council" and the number 352 on it,' said Mrs Drake. 'I suspect that there is quite a story behind this. You will all need to do some work to find out what this tag might be for. Now what else have we here? Ah, this takes me back.' She held up a large brown-coloured coin. 'Does anybody know what this is called?'

'Is it an old penny?' somebody said.

'That's right,' said Mrs Drake. 'And it looks like we have some stamps,' she said. 'Hands up those of you who collect stamps.'

Nobody put their hands up.

'Really, the study of philately is dying,' she said.

Everybody looked puzzled.

'Philately,' she said, 'is to do with the collecting and studying of postage stamps. Now, what else did the young Edith Emma Elliot leave for us to discover?'

There were two other items on the table.

'What's this?' asked Mickey as he held up a piece of round black plastic. It was about the same size as the penny.

'It's got something in white printed on it,' said Mrs Drake. 'Read it out loud, Mickey.'

'It says, "Engine Starting".'

'Well, that is a mystery,' said Mrs Drake. 'I've got no idea what that is. Now then, what is that folded paper? It looks like a page from a newspaper. Geraldine, perhaps you would like to investigate this for us.' She handed it to Geraldine.

Geraldine unfolded it and laid it flat on the table.

'It's the Daily Mirror,' said Geraldine, 'for 15 August 1945.' She read the headline out loud. '"Peace - Japan Surrenders - Allies Cease Fire". But I thought that happened on 2 September,' said Geraldine.

'That was when the formal surrender was signed,' said Mrs Drake. 'The fighting had stopped two weeks before on 15 August when there was a ceasefire declared.'

Everybody starting chatting as they looked at all the items on the table.

'Now, then children, this is all very exciting,' said Mrs Drake. 'We can learn a lot from the things which that young girl put in her time capsule. What I think we should do now is write an account of what we have discovered so far. You must write about the items and perhaps draw some pictures. You might also like to collect some more facts about the war. Feel free to handle the items and then go back to your table. Miss Rees will give out your exercise books to write in.'

Charlie picked up the piece of jagged metal and wondered why that was in the tin. He also picked up the round black piece of plastic with 'Engine Starting' written on it.

'What do you reckon that is?' asked Emma.

'I dunno,' said Charlie.

'It is exciting to actually handle things from history isn't it?' said Emma.

'I guess so,' said Charlie.

'Come on, let's go back to our table,' said Geraldine. 'We can start work on writing up our reports.'

'Yippee,' said Mickey.

They returned to their table and started to do some writing and drawing.

After a while Mrs Drake and Miss Rees walked around the class to see how everybody was getting on.

'You seem to all be working well,' said Mrs Drake as she came up to Charlie's table. 'Feel free to go to the library if you would like to find out some more facts about the war.' She then walked over to another table.

'That's a good idea,' said Geraldine. 'We can find out lots more in the library. Come on, let's take our exercise books and head up there.'

They started to make their way to the front.

Penny Elliot was sat at one of the tables they passed. Charlie reckoned she looked distracted. She didn't seem to be doing much writing.

'Penny, Mrs Drake says we can go to the library,' said Emma. 'Do you want to come with us?'

'Okay,' said Penny. She got up and joined them.

As they got to the front Mickey went over to the table with the tin and seemed to examine one of the items. Then he ran back to Charlie.

'What was that all about?' asked Charlie.

'Just wanted to handle history,' said Mickey.

With that, they walked out of the classroom and headed to the library.

'Woah look at the new furniture,' said Mickey as they walked in.

'I heard they were sprucing up the library,' said Geraldine. 'They're trying to make it a more fun place to learn.'

Mickey walked over to a long wooden seat with blue cushioning and sat on it. Charlie sat on one next to him. 'It's long enough to have a sleep on,' said Mickey, as he lay down. The he jumped up. 'And it's got a secret compartment', he said, 'well a drawer, anyway.'

The wooden panel at the front where their feet dangled had a hole at the top halfway along. The hole was the size of a hand. Mickey grabbed hold of it and pulled. 'Typical,' said Mickey. 'The drawer's jammed.'

'It's not a drawer,' said Charlie. 'This seat is a lid.' He got up, put his hand in the hole in his seat and pulled up the cushioned seat.

Mickey pulled his seat up too. 'Excellent, a hiding place,' said Mickey as they both looked at the big empty space.

'Why would you need to hide in the school library?' asked Charlie.

'Who knows?' said Mickey, as he closed the lid.

'Are you two going to do some work?' said Geraldine, who was browsing through some books on a bookshelf.

'Good point,' said Mickey. He then reached into his pocket and brought out the four marbles from the time capsule.

'What have you got them for?' asked Charlie.

'So I can handle history,' he said. He then threw them up into the air and went to catch them. But instead he dropped them and they scattered around the room. 'Oh, great,' said Mickey.

'Unbelievable,' said Geraldine, shaking her head, as she watched Mickey crawling around the floor and under furniture.

At that precise moment, Mrs Drake walked in. 'Mickey Dewhurst, why are you under that table?'

'I've lost my marbles.'

'That's one way of putting it,' said Geraldine.

'Very funny,' said Mickey.

'I want you all back in the classroom in ten minutes,' said Mrs Drake. 'Please use the time here profitably.' She then walked out.

'Come on, let's take these books on the war and go and sit at that table with Penny,' said Emma.

They all sat down at the table.

'Penny, are you alright?' asked Emma. 'You don't really seem with it. Are you tired of having to look after your mum?'

'No,' said Penny, 'it's not that.'

'Well, what's wrong?' said Emma.

'Nothing's wrong,' said Penny.

'Well, something's up,' said Emma.

'It's the time capsule,' said Penny. 'The person who made it and put all the things in it is still alive and living in Heatherbridge.'

'How do you know?' said Emma.

'Edith Emma Elliot is my great auntie.'

– CHAPTER 4 –

Dewhurst the dietician

They sat at the table in the library in stunned silence.

'Are you sure?' said Geraldine. 'It could be another girl with the same name.'

'It's definitely her,' said Penny. 'I remember her once saying to me that there was something secret buried on our school field. When I asked her what she meant she just smiled and said that it had to remain a secret. I thought she was just pulling my leg.'

'Good job she didn't tell you too, Charlie,' said Mickey. 'She might have pulled your artificial leg right off.'

'Grow up, Mickey,' said Geraldine.

'Why didn't you say something in the classroom?' asked Emma.

'I was too nervous,' said Penny. 'Anyway, I don't know if my auntie would want anybody to know it was her.'

'But she must know people would work it out,' said Geraldine.

'Maybe,' said Penny, 'but she didn't know when it would be found. Perhaps she thought it would be a long time after she had died.'

Then the door of the library burst open.

'What are you children doing?' It was Mrs Drake. 'I said ten minutes and you are still here, just talking, a quarter of an hour later. Geraldine Primrose, I would have thought at least you would have known better.'

'I'm sorry, Mrs Drake,' said Geraldine.

They sat there at the table in silence. Charlie felt a bit awkward. Nobody seemed to know what to say and do.

'I don't know what this is all about but I think somebody owes me an explanation,' said Mrs Drake.

Then Charlie heard the sound of sniffling and saw that Penny was crying.

'Mrs Drake,' said Emma, 'Penny has something to tell you.'

The following morning, straight after assembly, Charlie and his class walked out to the coach waiting in the school car park. Charlie sat next to Emma.

Mrs Drake was last to get on. As the door closed, she stood at the front and spoke to them. 'Now, children it is just a five-minute drive to the supermarket. Miss Rees has put all the fruit and vegetable costumes in the luggage compartment. When we arrive and get off will those dressing up please go to Miss Rees at the side of the coach and collect their costumes. The rest of you should all have your clipboards with your activity sheet on them.'

Charlie looked down at the sheet with questions about different types of foods and words to look out for on packages, such as *carbohydrates* and *vitamins*.

'You might like to familiarize yourself with the questions during the journey,' said Mrs Drake. 'Right, driver, we are ready when you are.' She sat down and the coach was soon leaving the school.

Charlie started to read through the questions but decided that could wait until they actually started the activity.

'Mickey seems a bit quiet,' said Emma, as the coach drove down the main road towards the supermarket.

Charlie looked up the aisle of the bus. Mickey was sitting two seats in front on the other side. He had his arms folded and looked fed up. 'I don't think he's looking forward to being dressed up as an orange,' said Charlie. 'I don't blame him, really.'

'I think he regrets volunteering,' said Emma.

'Yes,' said Charlie, 'he didn't really think about it. He just wanted to get out of doing maths.'

'I spoke to Penny before the bell went,' said Emma. 'She seemed alright about yesterday. She didn't seem to mind Mrs Drake telling the class about her auntie. What did you think about Mrs Drake's idea of some of us going with Penny to visit her auntie?'

'It's up to Penny, I s'pose,' said Charlie.

'I don't think she minds,' said Emma. 'I don't mind going with her. What about you?'

'It depends. I'm meant to be going to a climbing session at the High School sometime this week. Dad's taking me.'

'At the High School? What for?'

'They've got an indoor climbing wall. There's a climbing competition there a week on Saturday. I'm going there to do some practice.'

'A climbing competition? That's exciting. Have you got a chance of winning? I mean, what with your leg and everything.'

'Of course I have,' said Charlie, who felt a bit angry.

'Sorry, Charlie,' said Emma.

With that, the coach turned into Heatherbridge Supermarket car park.

As they all got off the coach Miss Rees, who was standing by the luggage compartment doors, said, 'Will the six who are wearing costumes please come and collect them.'

Charlie watched as Mickey and the other five children walked up to her.

'Now children, the rest of you follow me,' said Mrs Drake.

They walked across the car park and into the supermarket. They were greeted by a lady wearing a uniform.

'Good morning, everybody,' she said. 'My name is Louise. Welcome to Heatherbridge Supermarket. I am the assistant manager. The supermarket manager is busy at the moment but he hopes to say "hello" to you later.'

As she was speaking the six children carrying their costumes came in.

'This looks intriguing,' said the lady.

'They are costumes of various fruit and vegetables,' said Mrs Drake. 'We usually use a side office to put them on.'

'That's no problem,' said the lady. She called over to one of the shop assistants who was stocking some shelves. 'Sandra, can you take these children to the staffroom so that they can put their costumes on, please?'

Miss Rees and the children followed the assistant as she led the way to the staffroom.

'Now let me tell you a little about the supermarket,' said the lady.

The lady took them up one of the aisles, talking about different products on the shelves. This was useful because they were able to complete one or two questions on their clipboards.

Eventually, they reached the end of the aisle.

'Here we have the bakery section,' said the lady. 'As well as selling bread from other companies we also bake our own. As you can see, we have a wide range of things we bake ourselves such as multiseed cobs, pittas, tiger loaves, hot cross buns and cheese twists. We also sell plenty of bread flour.'

She pointed to a shelf full of packs of flour. A teenage assistant was there unloading some more.

'Careful with those bags, Joe,' said the lady. 'We don't want any accidents.'

The boy grunted and lifted another bag onto the pile.

'Right, I think you've a good idea of what we do at the supermarket,' said the assistant manager. 'Please feel free to wander around the shop to complete your activity sheets. Has anybody got any questions?'

One of the girls put her hand up.

'Yes,' said the lady.

'Why is that bread called tiger bread?'

'That's a good question,' said the lady.

'Perhaps somebody else in the class might like to suggest a reason,' said Mrs Drake.

Geraldine out her hand up.

'Yes, Geraldine,' said Mrs Drake.

'Because the person who first invented it thought it looked like the skin of a tiger,' said Geraldine.

'That's correct,' said the lady. 'Well done. This type of bread was first made in the Netherlands. Rice paste is applied to the outside before baking which gives it the mottled appearance.'

One of the boys put his hand up. 'Is there any lion bread?' he asked, with a smirk.

Geraldine huffed.

'No, there is no lion bread,' said the lady, laughing.

'We went to the wildlife park on Monday,' said Mrs Drake. 'We saw the enclosure for the lions they are expecting. Lions are the in thing at the moment amongst the class.'

'Oh, I read about the lions coming on their Facebook page,' said the lady. 'They're supposed to be arriving tomorrow.'

'Yes, they told us they were due on Thursday,' said Mrs Drake. 'But speaking of arrivals. I think the fruit and vegetables are approaching.'

They looked back towards the front of the shop. Walking up the aisle was Miss Rees followed by a carrot, a pineapple, a strawberry, a peapod and a parsnip. And behind all of them was an orange walking in zigzags and occasionally bumping into the shelves.

All the fruit and vegetables soon reached the rest of the class. All that is except the orange, which was still only halfway up the aisle.

'Miss Rees,' said Mrs Drake, 'I think you should go and take the top half of the orange off, at least until he reaches us.'

Miss Rees walked back down the aisle and removed the top half of the orange.

Mickey did not look very happy as he walked up the rest of the aisle. Some of the class were clapping, which Charlie reckoned only made him more unhappy. But he didn't try and stop them because he was clapping too.

'So much for anonumpty,' said Mickey, when he finally reached them.

'You mean anonymity,' said Geraldine, with a sigh.

'Whatever,' said Mickey.

'Well, this is quite a sight,' said the lady. 'You all look very impressive.'

'Their job is to encourage people to eat more fruit and vegetables,' said Mrs Drake.

'In that case, I will take them down to where we have the fruit and vegetables,' said the lady.

Then the carrot spoke. 'I can't see properly.'

The material had dropped over her eyes.

'Here, let me adjust it,' said Miss Rees. She put the top half of the orange down by the flour shelves and went over to the carrot.

And that's when Joe the assistant said, 'Oh no'.

Charlie turned round just in time to see a bag of flour dropping from the height of the top shelf. The assistant's arms were still stretched up above him as though he was still holding the bag. He seemed frozen in time. But the bag of flour was not frozen in time. It was plummeting downwards. But it didn't reach the floor. Instead, it landed on the top half of the orange.

'Oh, that's just great,' said Mickey. 'My orange is squashed.'

The orange now had a large dent in it the size of a flour bag.

'I'm really sorry,' said the assistant.

'It was my fault,' said Miss Rees, as she picked the bag out of the dent. 'I shouldn't have put it on the floor.'

'Look at it, it's ruined,' said Mickey. 'I'll have to stop being an orange.'

'No Mickey, you can still take part,' said Mrs Drake. 'At least now you can see where you are going. And you will be able to talk to customers more easily.'

'Yippee,' said Mickey.

'Right children, those in costumes go with Louise to the fruit and vegetable shelves. The rest of you can wander round the supermarket and work on your activity sheets.'

Charlie, Emma and Geraldine walked up and down the aisles together. Geraldine seemed to know all the answers and they soon had most of the activity sheet completed.

'Come on, let's go and see how Mickey is getting on,' said Emma.

'If we must,' said Geraldine.

They walked towards the fruit and vegetable shelves.

The children in costumes were all standing in a row. Mickey was on the end and looked miserable.

'Poor Mickey,' said Emma. 'He does look a bit funny with just the bottom half of the orange.'

'Serves him right for trying to dodge maths,' said Geraldine.

By now they had reached the shelves.

'How's it going, Mickey?' asked Charlie.

'How do you think it's going? I'm not happy. I look like half an orange, but I feel like a complete lemon.'

Then Mrs Drake appeared from round the corner. 'How are we all doing? Have you managed to speak to any customers yet? Ah, here comes a lady now.'

A lady was walking by pushing a shopping trolley.

'Madam, if you would like any advice about what to buy,' said Mrs Drake, 'please feel free to ask one of our fruit or vegetables.'

'Very well,' said the lady. 'Young man, what fruit and vegetables would you particularly recommend?' She was looking straight at Mickey.

'Well, uh, I um, would suggest you should eat all sorts of fruits,' said Mickey.

'And how should I prepare them?' said the lady. 'What's the best way to eat them?'

Charlie could see Mickey was trying to think hard about his answer. Charlie knew Mickey was concentrating because Mickey had clearly not noticed that the supermarket manager had come up behind him.

'Well, I think,' said Mickey that the best way to eat fruit is fruit jellies.'

'Fruit jellies?' said the lady. 'But they are sweets and covered in sugar.'

'Exactly,' said Mickey, with a grin.

Charlie saw that Mrs Drake looked worried and she looked like she was about to interrupt. But then the lady asked another question.

'And what vegetables would you recommend, young man?'

'Potatoes,' said Mickey.

'And what's the best way to eat them?' asked the lady.

'Crisps,' said Mickey.

'So young man you are suggesting that for a good all-round meal I should eat crisps and fruit jellies.'

'The ideal combination,' said Mickey.

'Well, that is certainly an unusual meal,' said the lady. 'But as it happens I do need to buy some potatoes and I might treat myself to some fruit jellies. Can you direct me to the correct shelves, please?'

'Oh, I wouldn't buy them here,' said Mickey. 'My mum reckons this place is expensive.'

The supermarket manager coughed.

Mickey looked behind him, looked back to the front and then gulped.

'Madam, I assure you that our prices are reasonable,' said the supermarket manager as he walked around in front of the row of children. 'And I am sure you will be able to buy all you need at Heatherbridge Supermarket for both a healthy diet and the occasional treat.'

'I do apologize,' said Mrs Drake. 'We are very grateful for you letting us visit your supermarket. The children always learn a lot.'

'Some have got a lot more to learn,' said the manager, 'especially this tulip.' With that he started to walk away.

'I'm not a tulip, I'm an orange,' shouted Mickey.

The supermarket manager kept walking, shaking his head.

'So much for anonymity,' said Geraldine.

'Come on,' said Emma. 'Let's find some more facts for our activity sheet.'

As the three of them were wandering around they bumped into Penny.

'Hi Penny,' said Emma. 'How are you getting on with the questions?'

'Not too bad. I've got about three to do'.

'Is there any news on meeting up with your great auntie?' asked Geraldine.

'I spoke to her on the phone last night. We can go and see her this evening about seven o'clock. But mum says I can only take three or maybe four with me.'

'I could come tonight,' said Geraldine.

'Me too,' said Emma. 'How about you Charlie?'

'I'd have to check first as I might be going climbing with Dad.'

'I suppose we ought to ask Mickey,' said Emma.

'This probably isn't the best time to ask him,' said Charlie. 'I'll ask him later when we get back to school.'

'I can't wait to meet her,' said Geraldine. 'I mean, what was that tag with a number?"

'And why put a jagged piece of metal in the time capsule?' said Emma. 'And what about the plastic with *Starting Engine* on it. What's that all about?'

They were right, thought Charlie. There were lots of questions to ask about the mysterious contents of the time capsule.

– CHAPTER 5 –

Auntie Edith explains

Charlie sat in the passenger seat clutching his piece of paper with the address.

'What's the exact address again?' said Father, as they stopped at some traffic lights.

'Twenty-three Linnell Road,' said Charlie.

'Linnell Road,' said Father. 'I think it's off that road to the left. Will you want me to take you right to the house?'

'No, we said we'd meet Penny by a bus stop a couple of doors down from her great aunt's house.'

'So how many are going?' said Father.

'Just Penny, Emma, Geraldine, and me.'

'No Mickey?' said Father, as the lights changed and he turned to the left.

'No, he didn't seem that keen. He said it would be boring.'

'But he was the one who found the time capsule, wasn't he?'

'Yeah, but he still didn't seem that bothered about coming.'

'I think this is Linnell Road coming up on the right,' said Father.

Charlie leant forward so he could read the road sign as soon as possible. 'Yeah, that's it,' he said, as the sign came into view.

They turned right and drove slowly down the road.

'There's the bus stop,' said Father. 'I'll pull up just before we get to it. Doesn't look like anybody is there yet.'

'We're early,' said Charlie as he looked at his watch. 'It's only five to seven.'

'This isn't actually that far from our home,' said Father. 'I think the park is down the other end of the road.'

'Yeah, it's not far.'

'That looks like them coming now,' said Father.

Charlie looked up and saw the three of them cycling up the road.

'Right, Charlie, don't forget, I've booked an hour's session on the indoor climbing wall at the High School for eight o'clock. Are you sure you've got everything? Your climbing shoes and harness and chalk bag?'

'Yeah, they're on the back seat.'

'Okay, I'll be outside number twenty-three at seven-forty-five prompt.'

'Thanks,' he said, as he opened the door.

'Have fun,' said Father.

'See you,' said Charlie. He got out and shut the door and his father drove off.

By now Penny, Geraldine and Emma were outside the gate to twenty-three. 'Hi, Charlie,' they said as he walked up to them.

'Hi,' said Charlie, as he realized he felt a bit awkward being the only boy. He wished Mickey had come too.

'Why didn't you cycle?' said Emma. 'It's not that far from your home.'

'I'm going for a climbing session at eight o'clock on the climbing wall at the High School,' said Charlie. 'Dad's picking me up at quarter to eight. It would have been a pain getting the bike into the car.'

'Quarter to eight?' said Geraldine. 'That's not very long. We had better hurry up.'

'I usually go down the side of the house and in the back way,' said Penny. 'We can take our bikes round the back. You can open the gate for us Charlie. It's never locked.'

Charlie walked ahead of them down a path by the side of the house. Halfway along was a tall wooden gate. He undid the latch and opened the gate. He pushed himself against the fence by next door's garden and held the gate as they all walked by pushing their bikes. Once they were all in, he closed the gate and walked behind them.

They soon reached the garden at the back. An old lady with a walking stick hanging from her arm was putting some bread on a bird table. It was on a sort of patio next to the house.

'Hello, Auntie Edith,' said Penny.

'Oh, hello, Penny dear.'

'These are my friends I told you about,' said Penny.

She introduced them to her Auntie.

'Well, it's very nice to meet you,' said Auntie Edith. 'Let me just finish putting this bread out then everything will be tickety-boo.'

Charlie looked at the garden. It was quite small. There was what looked like a piece of lawn but with very long grass. At the bottom of the garden was an old shed.

Auntie Edith must have seen Charlie looking. 'It's a bit overgrown,' she said, 'but at least the butterflies and bumblebees like it.'

'There's a red admiral over there,' said Geraldine. 'And a painted lady too.'

'Well spotted,' said Auntie Edith.

'This is a good garden for wildlife,' said Geraldine.

'I'm sure you are right, young lady,' said Auntie Edith, as she took hold of her walking stick. 'But I'd prefer it all completely tidy. Don't get me wrong, I love watching wildlife. But this garden does need some love and tender care. This little lawn needs relaying for a start. But I can only do so much. I've got loads of spades and forks and all sorts in the shed, but I'm afraid my joints are not what they used to be. Now then, to the matter in hand. A little bird tells me you have something to show me.'

'Yes, I've brought it with me,' said Penny, as she took off her backpack.

'All in good time, all in good time,' said Auntie Edith. 'But first let's go inside and I'll pour you all a nice glass of lemonade.' She turned to walk towards the backdoor then almost tripped up.

'Careful, Auntie,' said Penny as she reached out to hold her.

'These patio slabs are a little skew-whiff these days,' said Auntie Edith, pointing at them with her walking stick. 'Mind how you all go.'

Charlie watched his step, looking out for slabs that were sticking up, and went with everybody else into the house.

'Go through into the living room, my dears. I shall be with you presently.'

They walked into the living room. There were two armchairs and a settee. In the middle of the room was a coffee table. Charlie sat on an armchair and the three girls on the settee.

After a while Auntie Edith called out, 'Penny, dear, could you come and carry this tray in please?'

Penny went out and came back carrying a tray with four glasses of lemonade. She placed the tray on the coffee table.

'Help yourselves,' said Auntie Edith as she came in. She walked over to an armchair, sat down and placed her walking stick by her side.

They all sat there for a while sipping their lemonade.

'Now then, young Penny,' said Auntie Edith. 'I believe you have found the time capsule.'

'Well we didn't find it,' said Penny. 'A boy called Mickey Dewhurst found it. But he didn't want to come this evening.'

'He's probably very shy and quiet,' said Auntie Edith.

'Not exactly,' said Geraldine. 'When he found it he told everybody it was a bomb.'

'Did he indeed,' said Auntie Edith. 'Actually, there is an element of truth in that. Young Mickey was sort of right in one sense.'

'But it's a tennis ball tin,' said Geraldine.

'Indeed it is,' said Auntie Edith. 'But we are getting ahead of ourselves. Penny, I think you need to get out the time capsule.'

Penny took it out of the backpack and Auntie Edith held out her hands. Penny took it over to her and sat back down.

Auntie Edith turned it around and around. 'This is indeed my time capsule,' she said. 'Such young handwriting. I always prided myself on writing neatly.' She took a handkerchief out from the sleeve of her cardigan and dabbed her eyes. 'My my. Would you credit it? After all these years. Does it open easily?'

'Yes,' said Emma. 'It was difficult the first time but the top comes off easily now.'

'Emma,' said Auntie Edith. 'It is Emma, isn't it? Perhaps you would like to empty the contents onto the table. But first, why don't you bring the table closer to me.'

Emma got up and put the table right in front of Auntie Edith. She then took the tin off her. She removed the lid and allowed the contents to drop out, making sure as she did so that the marbles did not roll off the table.

'Ah, marbles,' said Auntie Edith. She leant forward and picked one up. 'Marbles was an important game when we were young. We all had a bag of marbles and played various games where you could win or lose some. These marbles are the small ones. There were larger ones too which were known as *kingers*. Now then, I had forgotten I had put these in.' She had picked up the stamps. 'Does anybody know what "1d" means?'

'It means one penny,' said Geraldine.

'That's correct,' said Auntie Edith. 'And of course, this is a one-penny coin,' she said as she pointed to the coin. 'And here we have a half-penny stamp, and a two-penny stamp. Does anybody know who the man is on the stamps?'

'Is he the king?' said Emma.

'Yes, that's right. He was King George the sixth. I can still remember his speeches on the radio. He had a stammer but he did very well.'

'Why did you put this toy car and tram in the time capsule?' asked Penny.

'To be honest I didn't really like toy cars,' said Auntie Edith. 'I can't really remember how I came to have them. I suppose I thought somebody in the future would be interested in them. Especially the tram.'

'I don't like cars much either,' said Geraldine. 'But it is fascinating.'

'Now does anybody know what this is?' asked Auntie Edith. She was holding the tag with the words "London County Council" and the number 352 on it.

'We don't really know,' said Geraldine.

'It was a tag worn by an evacuee.'

'What was an evacuee?' asked Emma.

'When the war started people were afraid that bombs would start falling on cities and major towns. So the government organized an evacuation of children who lived there to go and live in places where the bombing was unlikely. They were known as evacuees. They were put on trains with just a few possessions, including of course a gas mask, and they each wore a tag. The number refers to their particular school. On the back was their name and address but I think some tea or coffee spilt on this card so the name on the back has been lost.'

'Were you an evacuee?' asked Penny. 'Is it your card?'

'No,' said Auntie Edith. 'It was the tag belonging to a girl called Valerie who had come from London to live in Heatherbridge. She stayed with a family just down the road from me. She was my age and we became friends. One day she gave me the tag as a kind of present.'

'Did the children travel with their parents?' asked Emma.

'No, their parents stayed behind. It was very upsetting but the parents just wanted their children to be safe and many children saw it as an adventure. In early September 1939 one and a half million children were sent away. It took a lot of organizing. People from local authorities, teachers, railway staff and volunteers all helped. When they arrived at their destination they were taken to community halls and such like to be allocated a family to stay with. They stayed with these families for a long time until the bombing stopped. Although of course at first, during the so-called "phoney war" there was not much bombing and some parents started to get their children back home. But the government urged them not to because it knew bombing would eventually start. As of course it did.'

'Wasn't Heatherbridge bombed during the war?' asked Penny.

'No, hardly at all,' said Auntie Edith. 'There wasn't much to bomb here apart from the railway station. There were no big factories or anything like that. Also, the high mountains around the town made it more dangerous for aeroplanes, especially in the dark. So they tended to keep away from here. But one night some bombs did fall. They landed just at the edge of the town. An old barn was destroyed but nobody was hurt.'

'But why would they want to bomb a barn?' asked Emma.

'They weren't aiming for the barn,' said Auntie Edith, laughing. 'It was probably an enemy plane which had engine trouble or had been damaged by antiaircraft fire. It had not reached its target and decided to get rid of the bombs as soon as possible to lighten the load and to make it safer when it eventually landed.'

'But the bombs could have gone anywhere,' said Penny. 'They could have landed on your house.'

'I know,' said Auntie Edith. 'War is a terrible business. But, for us children, the next day it was very exciting. We all went to have a look at what happened. And some of us even found some fragments of the bombs. And that's what this piece of jagged metal is. I found it sticking into a tree near the barn. So you see, young Mickey was sort of right. It was a bomb buried in the ground, well, at least part of a bomb.'

'But what about this piece of plastic with "Engine Starting" on it?' asked Geraldine.

'Ah, now that was an exciting day too, at least for us children. One morning during our lessons at school we heard a loud bang. We ran to the window and could see a pall of smoke rising in the distance. Then we saw a man coming down from the sky by parachute. It turned out he had been flying a Spitfire which had been hit by gunfire from an enemy plane. He had baled out and his plane crashed into the ground. We went to the crash site after school. We weren't supposed to take anything but I found this piece of plastic. It was the cover over the button which started the engine.'

'Mickey will be amazed when we tell him,' said Emma.

'So much for him being a military expert,' said Geraldine. 'You'd think he would have known what it was.'

'This Mickey sounds a bit of a character,' said Auntie Edith.

'That's one way of putting it,' said Geraldine.

'Charlie, you've been very quiet,' said Auntie Edith. 'I'm sure you can spring to Mickey's defence.'

'He's a good laugh,' was all Charlie could think to say.

'Anyway, we've saved the best to last,' said Auntie Edith, as she unfolded the newspaper. '"Peace - Japan Surrenders - Allies Cease Fire"' she said as she read out the headline. 'That was certainly a happy day when we knew for sure that the world war was coming to end'. She took out her handkerchief again and dabbed her eyes. 'Well,' she said, 'I never thought I would see this time capsule again, but I must say it has brought back a lot of memories.'

'What are you going to do with your time capsule now?' asked Penny.

'I don't really regard it as mine,' said Auntie Edith. 'I buried it for somebody else to find. I think the best thing will be for it to be all put in a nice glass cabinet and put on display in your school.'

'That would be wonderful,' said Geraldine.

'Thank you,' said Emma.

Then they heard the hoot of car.

Charlie looked at his watch. It was quarter to eight. 'I'm sorry, I've got to go,' he said. 'That will be my dad outside. We're going climbing at the High School climbing wall.'

'Climbing?' said Auntie Edith. 'That does sound adventurous. Well, it's been nice to meet you, Charlie. Use the front door to leave, it will be quicker.'

Before he knew it Charlie was sitting in the car heading to the High School. He reckoned Mickey would be pretty annoyed that he had failed to identify a bomb fragment and the part of a Spitfire. But then Charlie's thoughts drifted to what lay ahead – the steep climbing wall with the large overhang.

– CHAPTER 6 –

The climbing wall

Charlie walked through the door into the sports hall, carrying his backpack. There were four separate games of badminton being played.

'It's a big sports hall isn't it?' said Father, who as well as a backpack was carrying a coil of rope.

'Yeah,' said Charlie, 'it's massive.'

'It must make the hall at your school seem really small.'

'Yeah, I guess so.' His father was right, he thought. And it wasn't just the sports hall. Everything at the High School seemed bigger than at Heatherbridge Junior School.

They stood for a moment watching the badminton players. Charlie felt a bit overawed and unsure of what to do.

'Right, never mind them,' said Father, 'we need to get climbing.' With that he turned to the left, walking down the side of the hall.

Charlie turned to follow him. It was then that he saw the climbing wall for the first time. It took up the middle third of the wall of the sports hall. He craned his neck upwards. The climbing wall seemed to go on and on towards the roof. But before it reached the roof the wall sloped outwards, almost horizontal, for several feet. This was the dreaded overhang. Even if he managed to reach the overhang, how was he, or anybody else, supposed to climb that?

A couple of climbers were already on the wall, each with another climber belaying them. Charlie and his father walked to a place below a clear part of the wall.

'Pretty impressive, don't you agree, Charlie?' said Father, as they both gazed upwards. 'It's got a great variety of holds, but most of them are those large easy looking holds, called jugs. There are some crimps and pinches too.'

'Which ones are they?' asked Charlie.

'The crimps are thin edges, just big enough for your fingers or the edge of your shoe. The pinches are those tiny holds which you literally have to pinch hold of with your thumb and fingers.'

'What are those large round ones near the top, just below the overhang?' asked Charlie. 'They don't look like holds at all.'

'They're called slopers,' said Father. 'They basically slope away from the wall and are mostly just smooth. To use them you have to place the whole of both hands on them. You use a lot of muscle groups, not just finger strength. They're for advanced climbers, mind. You'll need to have a lot of practice and patience before you climb them. Okay, we don't want to go and injure ourselves so let's warm up first.'

Charlie knew what he had to do because his father had taught him to do this before every climb. They both jogged on the spot for a minute or so. Once Charlie began to feel out of breath he stopped and did some stretching exercises.

The final part of the warm-up involved putting their rock shoes on and making a few basic climbing moves just a couple of feet off the ground.

'Okay,' said Father, as they both jumped off some holds, 'I think we're warmed up enough. Let's get ready.'

Charlie went over to his backpack and took out the climbing harness. Once he had attached his chalk bag to the back of the top belt, he put his legs though the loops, pulled up the harness and buckled the waist belt, making it double secure by doubling the belt back through the buckle. 'Who's going first?' asked Charlie.

'You go first, Charlie,' said Father. 'Here, tie this to your harness.'

Charlie took the rope and tied a figure-eight knot about two and a half feet off from the end. He threaded the two and a half feet of excess rope through the loop on the leg belt and the loop on the waist belt. He then pulled it until the knot was a few inches from his belt. He passed the excess rope through the figure-eight knot, following the line of the knot so that he ended up with a double figure-eight knot, known as the climber's knot. He then tied a stop knot at the end of the excess rope.

While Charlie had been doing this, his father was passing the other end of the rope through the belay device which he had attached to his own harness.

'Right,' said Father, 'let's check you're ready. By the way have you remembered to put a chalk ball in the chalk bag and not loose chalk?'

'Yes,' said Charlie. He put his hand behind his back and lifted the chalk ball out of his chalk bag. A chalk ball is really just a very small sealed bag with chalk packed inside, but the bag is porous allowing chalk to come through its sides when you squeeze the bag.

'Good,' said Father, as he looked at the bag. 'Indoor climbers don't like a lot of dust around. Okay, let's do the check. Harness is double-backed, rope goes through both belts, knot a fist's width from the harness, double figure-eight correctly tied and the excess rope has a stop knot. Okay, well done Charlie, you're good to go.'

Charlie moved up to the wall and looked upwards.

'Every so often there are quickdraws hanging from the wall,' said Father.

'You mean those things looking like carabiners,' said Charlie.

'Yes, a quickdraw is basically two carabiners linked together by a few inches of semi-rigid material. One carabiner is attached to a bolt on the wall. The other carabiner is the one you put your rope through. Just push the rope against the gate and it will easily go in. Then the gate will snap shut. It's just like when you attach carabiners to protection you've put in while climbing on rock. Anyway, every time you come to one, pass your rope through it. That way, you will not fall very far if you come off.'

'Okay,' said Charlie. He put his good foot on a hold low down near the ground. Then he reached up with his arms outstretched and grabbed hold of two good holds. 'Climbing,' he said. He lifted up his artificial leg and put the foot on a large hold to the right. With that, he was on his way.

The climbing was easy to start with and there were plenty of holds.

'As it's your first time on this wall don't worry about using any particular coloured hold,' said Father. 'Just use any one you feel like.'

After only a few moves Charlie came to the first quickdraw. It was about level with his eyes and just to the left. 'Slack,' shouted Charlie.

'Okay,' said Father, as he belayed a few extra feet of rope.

Charlie reached down, grabbed the rope, pulled it up and pushed it into the quickdraw. The gate on the quickdraw snapped shut again with a reassuring click. He saw the rope tighten as his father then pulled back the slack. Charlie then pressed on up the wall.

'You're going well,' shouted Father.

Then Charlie, rather than reaching higher up, grabbed just a few inches further up.

'Keep your arms straight, Charlie,' shouted Father.

As soon as he had made the move Charlie knew it was not the best. By reaching up just a few inches his arm was now bent. It was already starting to ache with the increased effort from his arm muscles this position required. Also, by bending his arm his centre of gravity was being forced away from the wall.

'Come on' muttered Charlie. He let go of the hold and with the same hand reached up to a higher hold. With his arm now straight he felt himself move closer to the wall. 'Take in' shouted Charlie.

'Taking in,' shouted Father.

Charlie felt the rope tighten. He didn't think he was about to fall but he knew he had to gather his thoughts for a moment. He heard somebody cheer from below. He glanced down. A pair had just won a particularly important point in a badminton game. Charlie turned once more to the wall inches in front of his face. 'Concentrate,' he muttered, as he reached behind his back and rolled the chalk ball around in his hand to give extra grip.

'Hip to the wall,' shouted Father.

Charlie glanced down at his feet. They were both pointing to the wall. He carefully turned his artificial right foot sideways. He felt his right hip touch the wall.

Immediately he felt more comfortable as his centre of gravity was now pressing down more on the footholds rather than trying to pull him off the wall. Being side-on close to the wall also gave him a longer reach. With his right hand, he grabbed for a handhold which was now just within his range above his head.

'Use your feet, Charlie.'

'I am,' shouted Charlie who was getting a bit annoyed with the constant stream of advice from below. Of course, he knew his father was right. The golden rule of climbing is that you support your weight as far as possible with your feet, not your hands. The hands are supposed to be just for balance. Charlie knew this would go out the window when it came to the overhang. But that still seemed far away.

Then he heard somebody shout.

'Watch me! Take in!'

Charlie glanced up to his right. It was a climber who had reached halfway across the overhang. But he was obviously struggling.

'You can do it,' shouted the man who was belaying him. 'You can send it.'

Charlie knew that to send a route was climbing jargon for completing a route. But Charlie didn't think the climber looked at all like he was going to send the route. Not this time anyway.

'Watch me,' shouted the climber again.

Then Charlie sensed that something wasn't right. He couldn't work it out at first. Then he realized what was wrong. The rope from the man was not connected to a quickdraw on the overhang or even near the overhang. The last one he had used was several feet below the overhang. But there was nothing Charlie could do.

For a few more moments the man hung on. Then he shouted 'falling' and fell like a stone from the overhang. He fell vertically at first, but eventually, the rope caught him. But now he was swinging in towards the wall. He came to a sudden halt as he crashed against a sloper.

'You alright?' shouted the belayer.

'Yeah,' shouted the climber after a few seconds.

'You wanna try again?' said the belayer.

'No,' said the climber.

'Okay, lowering,' said the belayer.

The climber slowly descended, occasionally kicking himself away from the wall to avoid protruding holds.

Charlie took a deep breath and carried on climbing. As soon as he could he pushed his rope into the next quickdraw he came to.

'You're doing good,' shouted his father.

Charlie kept going and noticed that the holds were becoming fewer. And the ones that were there were smaller and more difficult to stand on and hold. But as he pushed his rope into yet another quickdraw and looked up he realized that the holds immediately above were now much larger. But this was not good news. These were the slopers.

'You ready to come down, Charlie?' shouted his father.

'Not yet,' said Charlie. 'I want to reach the overhang.'

'Don't overdo it.'

Charlie put each hand in turn into his chalk bag and chalked them up. Then he reached up with his right hand and tried to get a grip on the nearest sloper. But his hand slipped off. There seemed to be no grip at all. By now his arms and legs were aching. He knew the lactic acid would be building up in his muscles. He didn't have much time left.

'Try both hands,' shouted Father, who didn't sound very hopeful.

'Watch me!' shouted Charlie. He reached up with his right hand and as soon it touched the sloper he moved his left hand up. He craned his neck but all he could see were his hands slowly slipping off the sloper. 'Falling!' he shouted.

'Got you,' shouted Father.

Charlie's hands slipped right off the sloper. He fell backwards into space, but was soon caught by the rope. He swung back and forth like a pendulum until he managed to stop himself by grabbing a hold. He steadied himself and got his feet onto some holds. He then dangled each arm in turn to try to ease the aching. He looked back up at the sloper. He toyed with the idea of climbing back up a few feet to have another go. But he knew it would be a waste of time.

'You ready to come down?' shouted Father.

'Yes,' shouted Charlie.

'Okay, lowering.'.

As Charlie slowly descended he looked back up at the receding slopers. How am I supposed to climb the overhang if I can't get to it in the first place? thought Charlie.

Charlie kept opening and closing his fists as they drove home.

'Are your fingers still aching?'

'Yeah, a bit,' said Charlie.

'What did you make of the wall?' asked Father.

'Those slopers are impossible.'

'Yeah, they're pretty tough,' said Father. 'We should be able to get another practice in before the competition.'

'But they might change the layout for the competition,' said Charlie.

'In theory, it should all be changed,' said Father, 'but it's only a local competition and no one's got time to do that. Anyway, it belongs to the school and they probably wouldn't agree to it being changed. I shouldn't imagine they have got any spare holds for a start.'

'Even if I get passed the slopers I'll still need to climb the overhang,' said Charlie. 'I'm sure at least some of the other climbers in my age group will be able to do that. I have never climbed an overhang.'

'Don't worry. We'll get you some overhang practice one way or another,' said Father.

They drove along in silence for a while.

'Any news on those lions coming to the wildlife park?' said Father.

'The man said they were coming on Thursday,' said Charlie.

'That's tomorrow,' said Father.

'Yeah.'

Father put the car radio on and hummed to the music on the local station. Then the music stopped.

'Just a reminder about the weather for tomorrow,' said the man on the radio. 'The Met Office are warning of stormy weather in our region, especially the afternoon. So batten down the hatches, Heatherbridge.'

'Hmm, not exactly ideal weather for lions,' said Father.

– CHAPTER 7 –

Searching for thruppence

'Get to your places and settle down,' said Mrs Drake as they returned from assembly the following morning.

Miss Rees was finishing putting maths exercise sheets on the tables.

As they were sitting down Charlie saw Mickey going up to Mrs Drake and speaking to her.

'What is he doing now?' said Geraldine.

'I dunno,' said Charlie.

Then Mickey came to their table with a big grin and sat down.

'What's going on?' asked Charlie.

'Operation Delay Maths is about to begin,' said Mickey. 'Sit back and watch the expert at work.'

'Now, children, we must carry on with our multiplication and division exercises this morning,' said Mrs Drake. 'What with visiting the wildlife park and the supermarket, useful though they were, we are getting behind with our maths.'

'Mrs Drake is right,' said Geraldine to Charlie and the others on the table. 'We are getting behind.'

'Brace yourself, Geraldine,' said Mickey. 'It's about to get a lot worse.' He grinned at Charlie and gave a thumbs up.

'This afternoon we will do some more work on our little time capsule project,' said Mrs Drake. 'I understand Penny went with Geraldine, Emma and Charlie to visit Penny's great auntie yesterday evening. They will be able to explain to us more about the items which we couldn't identify. But for something to whet our appetite for this project work, Mickey tells me he has something important to show the class. Apparently, it is to do with the time capsule. He says it is so fascinating it cannot possibly wait until this afternoon. So Mickey, would you like to come to the front?'

'Yes, of course,' said Mickey. But instead of getting up straight away, he brushed his hair with his hands. 'How do I look?' he said to Geraldine.

'Just get on with it,' said Geraldine.

'Mickey please hurry up,' said Mrs Drake.

Then Mickey coughed and banged his chest. 'I might need a glass of water,' he said. 'Shall I go and get one from the dinner ladies in the kitchen?'

'Mickey, please come to the front and show the class what you have brought,' said Mrs Drake.

Mickey got up and walked towards the front of the classroom. When he had got about halfway, he stopped and looked out the window. 'It's such a fine day, today,' he said. 'If only we could go outside and enjoy the sunshine.'

'It's not going to last,' said a boy nearby. 'My dad says there is a bad storm forecast for this afternoon.'

'Yes, I heard that too,' said Mickey, as he folded his arms, leant backwards and half sat on the table he was standing by. 'It's going to be bad,' he said, shaking his head.

'Mickey Dewhurst will you please get to the front,' said Mrs Drake.

'What?' said Mickey, as though surprised. 'Sorry, I was miles away.'

'Mickey, please,' said Mrs Drake.

'He's just trying to delay maths,' said Geraldine. 'He probably hasn't got anything worth showing.'

'I have,' said Mickey. 'You'll be astounded.'

'Mickey, we shall all be astounded if you manage to get to the front,' said Mrs Drake.

Eventually Mickey reached the front. He turned around, faced the class, and stood with his hands in his pockets.

'Well, go on,' said Mrs Drake.

'You want me to begin?' said Mickey.

'Mickey Dewhurst, take your hands out of your pockets, stand up straight and show the class what you have brought.'

Mickey coughed then started to pace back and forth with his hands behind his back. 'You will remember that we found a time capsule,' he said. 'I knew straight away it was something from the time of the Second World War because …'

'Mickey, show us what you have brought, or go and sit down,' said Mrs Drake.

'Well, actually there's a problem,' said Mickey.

'What do you mean, there's a problem?' said Mrs Drake.

'Well, you told me to take my hands out of my pockets. But what I've got to show is in my pocket. So I'll have to put a hand back in my pocket.'

Mrs Drake just glowered at him.

Mickey seemed to be frightened by this. He put his hand in his pocket. First, he pulled out a handkerchief.

'This is gross,' said Geraldine.

Then he took a small object out of his pocket and put his handkerchief back. He held the object up to the class between his finger and his thumb. 'Does anybody know what this is?' he asked.

'It's obvious,' said a boy at the back. 'It's a coin.'

'Yes, but what kind of coin?' said Mickey.

'Mickey, unless I am mistaken, that is an old thruppenny bit,' said Mrs Drake. 'Worth three old pennies.'

'That's correct,' said Mickey.

'And what has that got to do with the time capsule?' asked Mrs Drake.

'It's got 1943 on it,' said Mickey. 'It's from the Second World War. My mum was given it by my great-grandpa. She said I could show it to everybody.'

'Well Mickey it certainly is interesting,' said Mrs Drake. 'Thank you for bringing it in. Now please return to your seat and let's start work on our maths.'

Mickey put the coin back in his pocket and walked back to his table. 'Well, I delayed it a bit,' he said, as he sat down.

'I thought it was interesting,' said Emma.

Geraldine sighed and started to work on the exercise sheet.

Charlie started to work on the sums and found them quite tricky. Perhaps Mickey had the right idea, he thought.

'Thank you for explaining everything to the class, Geraldine,' said Penny.

It was the middle of the afternoon and most of the class were in the library finding out facts about the Second World War.

'That's okay,' said Geraldine. 'It made sense for just one of us to speak.'

'I always get nervous doing that kind of thing,' said Penny.

'Me too,' said Emma. 'What about you, Charlie?'

'I don't like speaking in front of the whole class,' said Charlie.

'There's nothing to it,' said Mickey. 'You've just got to have something to talk about.' He took the thruppenny bit out, tossed it into the air, and then put it back in his pocket.

'Your hopeless,' said Geraldine, as she sighed.

'Thanks a lot,' said Mickey.

'I thought your great auntie was a lovely old lady,' said Emma.

'Thank you,' said Penny.

'We ought to do something for her,' said Emma.

'What do you mean?' said Geraldine.

'Well, she went to the trouble of making up the time capsule in the first place. And she explained everything to us last night. We should do something.'

'Like what?' said Geraldine.

'I don't know. Get her some chocolates. Buy some flowers. Something anyway. What do you think, Charlie?'

'Yeah, sounds like a good idea.'

'What?' said Emma. 'What's a good idea? The flowers? Chocolates?'

'Whatever,' said Charlie, who didn't really feel like coming up with any suggestions.

'You're a big help, Charlie,' said Emma. 'I just thought it would be nice to do something for her.'

'I can't think of anything at the moment,' said Charlie.

'You're hopeless,' said Emma.

'Welcome to the club, Charlie,' said Mickey.

'Just because I can't think of an idea at this precise moment does not mean I'm hopeless,' said Charlie, who felt annoyed. He was also feeling tired after the climb last night.

'My great auntie really wouldn't expect anything,' said Penny. 'Please don't worry about it.'

'We need to do some work,' said Geraldine. 'We can't just sit at this table all day.'

'Anyway, why has this table got a plastic vase of flowers on it?' said Mickey.

'I think they're trying to make it all look nice for this evening,' said Geraldine.

'What do you mean?' asked Emma. 'What's happening this evening?'

'They're doing an open evening for parents of children in the final year of the infant school who will be coming here in September,' said Geraldine. 'It was on our school website. Starts at 7.30.'

It was then that the first flash of lightning lit up the whole room.

Emma screamed. She pushed against the table and the vase began to tip over.

Charlie grabbed it before it fell over but some water splashed onto the table.

'I knew this handkerchief would come in useful,' said Mickey. But as he pulled it out of his pocket there was a massive crash of thunder.

They all jumped.

'Whoa, that was close,' said Mickey as he wiped the table.

Then they heard the rain crashing against the windows. Meanwhile, there was another flash of lightning followed even more quickly by a roll of thunder which echoed around the sky.

One or two of the children were crying.

Then Mrs Drake came in. 'Come on children, let's all get back to the classroom.'

'It's impossible to concentrate with all the noise,' said Geraldine.

They were sat around the table trying to read their books.

'You must be glad you're not in the mountains climbing at the moment, Charlie,' said Emma.

'Yeah, it would be pretty scary,' he said, as another flash of lightning lit up the clouds.

They carried on reading for a few more minutes. Then, one of the boys stood up, pointing towards the window. 'Look, it's the lions coming.'

Charlie looked through the window to the road that ran by the school. Sure enough, there was a lorry driving by with South Downs Safari Park on its side.

'Those poor lions,' said Emma, as they stood up to look. 'They must have had an unpleasant journey. They will be glad to get to Heatherbridge Wildlife Park.'

'Come on children, let's get back to our reading,' said Mrs Drake.

For the rest of the afternoon they concentrated as best they could, but Charlie was glad when it was time to go. As he stepped outside he had to dodge some puddles, but the rain had stopped and the sun was shining.

Charlie had only just finished dinner when his phone went off. It was a text from Mickey.

'Emergency. Can you meet on bike at park in 15 min?'

'Mum, its Mickey,' said Charlie. 'He wants to meet me at the park. Can I go?'

'I suppose so,' she said. 'Be sure to be back by 7.30.'

'Okay, thanks,' said Charlie. He texted back 'yes' to Mickey and then set off.

When he got to the park Mickey was waiting by the entrance.

'What's the emergency?' asked Charlie.

'I've lost the thruppence,' said Mickey.

'What? In the park? You'll never find it.'

'No, not the park,' said Mickey. 'I think it's in the school. The library to be precise.'

'But you had it in the library,' said Charlie. 'I remember you taking it out of your pocket. And you put it back in your pocket afterwards.'

'Exactly. But that's the last time I remember having it. I think it may have come out of my pocket when I took the handkerchief out to wipe up the water when that vase tipped up.'

'So why have you come to the park?' asked Charlie.

'This is just a place to meet. We need to go to the school.'

'What do you mean *we*? It's nothing to do with me. Anyway, if it's there you can get it tomorrow.'

'A cleaner or somebody might find it or even vacuum it up without realizing it. I need you to help me look for it. If I lose it I'll be in big trouble at home.'

'You lost it a long time ago,' said Charlie.

'Very funny,' said Mickey.

'Anyway,' said Charlie, 'the place will be all locked up.'

'No, there's that open evening thingy going on. They'll be showing people around and everything. Every door will be unlocked. If we go now we can get in there, find it and get out before they arrive. All we'll need to do is dodge the caretaker. We'll hide our bikes in the bushes near the side entrance and go in that way.'

'No way,' said Charlie. 'It'll never work.'

'Please Charlie. You should be honoured I'm allowing you to come on one of my missions.'

'I'm overwhelmed,' said Charlie. 'I've got to be back by seven-thirty. We haven't got enough time.'

'Of course we have,' said Mickey. 'We'll be out by seven. If we leave it any later the place will be swarming with teachers and parents. Come on. Let's go.' With that Mickey turned his bike around and headed off down the path.

Charlie hesitated for a moment and then raced after him. Within five minutes they careered into the school car park. Charlie could see the main door of the school was propped open. Somebody was standing in the reception area but had their back to the door. Charlie followed as Mickey rode around the side of the school.

Mickey leapt off his bike and put it between a bush and the wall of the school.

Charlie hid his bike too.

'Come on,' said Mickey.

Before he knew it Charlie was running into the side entrance and down a corridor to the library.

But as they ran they heard police sirens blaring.

'What's all that about?' said Charlie.

'Who knows?' said Mickey. 'Keep running.'

'I told you everything would be open,' said Mickey as they reached the library. 'Even the library door is wedged open.'

Charlie glanced down at the wooden wedge jammed under the door.

'Isn't it supposed to stay shut?' said Charlie. 'It's a fire door.'

'Never mind that,' said Mickey. 'We need to start looking. Right, I was sitting here, I took my handkerchief out and … there it is! Found it! Right, we need to get out of here.'

But Charlie wasn't looking at Mickey. He was looking out of the window. 'Mickey, get down!'

'Uh?'

Charlie had dived to the ground. 'Get down, Mickey!'

Mickey lay down. 'What's wrong?' he said.

'Look,' said Charlie. Charlie was peeking over the windowsill.

Mickey crawled over to the window and peeked too.

There were police cars and Land Rovers and men with rifles pointing at the school.

'What's happening?' said Charlie.

'It's obvious,' said Mickey. 'They've heard I'm in here and they know that's the only way they can take me out.'

'Don't be ridiculous,' said Charlie, trembling, as he got his phone out.

'Who're you gonna phone?' asked Mickey. 'Don't you think we should stay quiet?'

'I'm not phoning anybody,' said Charlie. 'I'm trying to get the local radio station to find out what's going on.'

Charlie eventually managed to find the radio station and they sat and listened to the announcer.

'So just to recap on our breaking story. A lorry carrying lions to Heatherbridge Wildlife Park crashed when it hit a landslide caused by the storm. The driver and lions were unharmed. But the male lion, Mason, the head of the pride, escaped. He has just been seen running across Heatherbridge Junior School's playing field and is believed to be in the school, whose doors were open ready for an open evening. The few staff who were on site are hiding in the head teacher's study with the door locked and barricaded. Police are urging the general public and children to keep well away from the school.'

'Oh that's just great,' said Mickey. 'The police are pleading with children to keep away from the school. And where am I? In the school.'

'Mickey, what we going to do? It could attack us.'

'It won't come here,' said Mickey. 'It will head for the kitchen where the food is. There is no reason for a lion to come to the library.'

'I can think of two reasons,' said Charlie.

'What?' said Mickey.

Charlie just looked at Mickey.

Then Mickey's face went white. 'You mean ...?' He pointed at Charlie. Then he pointed at himself. Then he gulped.

'We need to get out of here,' said Charlie.

They both half-crawled, half-ran to the library entrance. They poked their heads around the doorway. They both gasped. There padding down the corridor towards them and gathering speed all the time, was Mason, the African lion.

– CHAPTER 8 –

Lightbulb moment

They both pulled their heads back into the library
'Do you think he saw us?' said Mickey.
'Of course he did,' said Charlie.
'We need to run for it.'
'We'll never make it,' said Charlie, as he started to kick the wedge with his foot. 'We need to stay in here.'
'What are you playing at? Just close the door!'
'The wedge is jammed,' said Charlie. 'It won't budge.'
Then they heard a loud roar.
'What are we going to do?' said Mickey.
Charlie looked back into the library. 'Of course!' he said. 'Those new long wooden seats with the hidden storage space.'
They ran over to the seats which were next to each other.
There was another roar.
'He's getting closer,' said Mickey.
Charlie lifted up the seat and was about to dive in. But then he stopped. 'No way!' he said. 'It's full of books!'
'Mine too,' said Mickey as he lifted his seat.
They both began scrabbling in the storage spaces, throwing out the books behind them to make enough room to get in.
Then Mickey threw one of the books towards the door. 'That'll annoy him,' he said.

'Why?' asked Charlie.

'It's *Born Free* by Joy Adamson.'

'That's hilarious Mickey. Anyway, what are you trying to annoy him for?'

There was another roar, loud and right outside the door.

'Get in!' said Charlie.

Charlie dived into the storage space, landing on the few remaining books. He pulled the seat down and it closed with a bang. He heard Mickey's seat close too. Then there was silence.

Charlie looked through the tiny gap in the front of the panel of the seat. It was there to allow somebody's hand to get under the top of the seat to lift it. If the lion worked out how to lift the seats, Charlie knew they would be in real trouble.

'Has he come in?' whispered Mickey.

'Keep quiet,' said Charlie as he moved his head to the side of the gap so he could look towards the door. Perhaps the lion had decided to keep walking down the corridor. Then Charlie saw a shadow fall on the floor of corridor. The next moment the doorway was filled by the head and mane of Mason the African lion.

Charlie moved back from the gap and lay down, hardly daring to breathe.

There was only one sound, the sound of paws padding along the floor. The sound was getting closer and closer.

But then there was another sound, coming from way in the distance, outside. It was the sound of a slow-moving vehicle and a man speaking on a tannoy. 'This is the police. Will people please remain inside their homes and keep their doors and windows closed. There is no need to be alarmed.'

'That's easy for him to say,' whispered Mickey.

Then Charlie's storage space went absolutely pitch black. Charlie looked towards the gap. All he could see was a large eye staring at him.

Charlie lay as still as he could. Could the lion see him inside the dark box? Charlie had no idea. But what he did know was that the unblinking eye was not moving and was looking straight in his direction. Then the eye moved away. For a moment Charlie could only see books and shelves. Maybe the lion had gone. But then there was a loud roar and a scraping, screeching sound as the claws of the lion scraped along the front of the storage space.

'He's trying to break into the storage space!' said Charlie

'And he's ruining the books,' said Mickey.

Charlie was annoyed that Mickey didn't seem concerned about the lion breaking into his storage space. But Mickey was right, thought Charlie, as he saw the lion take a step away from the seat and trample all over the books they had thrown out.

But then Charlie heard Mickey gulp.

The lion had moved towards the gap in the front panel of Mickey's seat.

'Nice little lion,' said Mickey, who sounded terrified.

The lion roared and lifted one of his paws. There was a loud bang. Charlie reckoned he must have opened Mickey's seat a fraction only for it to come crashing back down.

'He's trying to open it,' said Mickey.

Charlie watched through the gap. The lion stepped back from Mickey's seat. He stood there looking down at it for what seemed an age. Charlie thought he might be gathering himself to make a full-blown attack on Mickey's seat.

'Nice little lion, nice little lion,' Mickey kept repeating.

But then the lion seemed to lose interest in the seat. He moved back and looked out towards the window and just stood still.

Charlie looked away from the gap. He was getting a headache from just staring all the time while bent double.

Then Mickey said, 'Oh no, not in the library. Naughty lion.'

'What's happening?' asked Charlie. But before Mickey could answer there was a plopping sound.

'That is really going to annoy Geraldine,' said Mickey. 'It's landed smack on top of an advanced maths book. Maybe this lion isn't so bad after all.'

It was then that the smell reached the compartments.

'Woah, that is gross!' said Mickey.

Charlie coughed, waving his hand up and down in front of him. 'Where ... where is he now?' said Charlie.

'He's gone down town to buy some air freshener,' said Mickey. 'He's in the library, where do you think he is?'

'Yes, but where exactly? Is he heading towards the door?'

'I think he's over by the history section,' said Mickey. 'He needs to get out more.'

'That's what he's done,' said Charlie. 'He's got out.'

'Very funny,' said Mickey. 'Hang on, he's making a move.'

Charlie looked through the gap. The lion was walking towards the doorway. 'Keep going,' muttered Charlie. Then he stopped.

'What's he stopped for?' said Mickey.

'He's sniffing that book you threw at him,' said Charlie.

'I didn't throw it at him,' said Mickey. 'I just thought he might enjoy reading it.'

'You said it would annoy him,' said Charlie. 'Anyway, the point is, he's stopped going out.'

But then the lion huffed, left the book behind and walked out into the corridor.

'He's heading back the way he came,' said Charlie.

'What do we do now?' said Mickey.

'We need to sit tight for a few minutes. We can't get out yet in case he comes back.'

'This is a nightmare,' said Mickey. 'Not only am I trapped at school, I'm trapped in the library at school. And not only am I trapped in the library at school, but I'm also trapped in a box in the library at school.'

'It could be worse,' said Charlie, 'You could have been eaten by a lion.'

'I don't think he's that dangerous anyway,' said Mickey. 'He wasn't particularly scary.'

'Yeah, right,' said Charlie. 'That's why you kept saying *nice little lion.*'

'Exactly, he's nice and little.'

'You were scared stiff,' said Charlie.

'Anyway, never mind that,' said Mickey. 'Can we get out now?'

'No, we need to wait a few more minutes.'

'I thought you had to get back home,' said Mickey.

'Yeah, by seven thirty.'

'It's five past now,' said Mickey.

'No way,' said Charlie. He held his wrist up to the gap and looked at his watch. 'Maybe we could try now.' He slowly lifted the seat and peered out.

The library was a shambles. There were books strewn across the floor where they had been thrown out. There were other books which had been knocked off the shelves by the lion as he had wandered around.

Charlie crept over to the doorway and peered out. There was no sign of the lion. He looked back into the library and saw Mickey climbing out of the storage space. Then he heard voices from outside.

'He's coming out the doorway,' somebody shouted.

Charlie and Mickey ran to the window, keeping low as they did so. They watched as the lion walked out of the school reception into the car park.

'Fire tranquillizer,' somebody shouted.

There was a small bang. The lion took a couple more steps then lay down on the tarmac.

'That's him out for the count,' said Mickey.

Some men in wildlife park uniforms walked slowly towards the lion, pointing their rifles at him. Then others ran forward carrying a large tarpaulin. Meanwhile, a flatbed truck with a cage was being reversed into the car park.

'I thought everybody was supposed to be inside,' said Mickey, as a large crowd began to gather outside the school gates.

By now the lion had been lifted onto the tarpaulin.

Charlie looked at his watch. It was ten past seven. 'I need to get going,' he said. 'How are we going to get out of the school without anybody noticing?'

'We'll use the crowd,' said Mickey. He pointed at the people who had now come through the gates and were surrounding the lorry, taking pictures with their phones.

'What do you mean, *use the crowd*?' said Charlie. 'They'll all see us.'

'Look, the crowd is getting bigger and bigger,' said Mickey. 'Give it another couple of minutes then we can just merge in with them. No one will ever know we've been inside here.'

'Except there are all these books,' said Charlie. 'We'd better put them back.'

'It's okay,' said Mickey. 'They'll just blame the lion. Anyway, do you wanna touch *that*?' He was pointing at the advanced maths book, which was almost completely covered with the big dollop of muck left by the lion.

'Okay,' said Charlie. 'Let's get down to the side door.' But then something caught Charlie's eye. 'That's it!' he said.

'What's it?' said Mickey.

Charlie picked up a book and read out the title. '"Make Your Grandparent's Garden Great – Top Tips for Gardening Grandkids"'.

'What's that got to do with the price of bread?' said Mickey.

'Don't you see? Emma was on about doing something for Penny's great auntie. You know, because she took the trouble to explain the time capsule and everything.

'So?' said Mickey.

'We could tidy up her garden for her.'

'How bad is the garden? It's not that bad, is it?'

'If you had gone you would have seen it,' said Charlie.

'Ouch, got me there. Anyway, that book will be no use. It's for gardens of grandmas not great aunties.'

'The book's not the point. It's the idea. It's what Geraldine would call a lightbulb moment.'

'I'm no expert,' said Mickey. 'But if you're gonna plant some bulbs, don't use lightbulbs.'

'Anyway,' said Charlie as he threw the book back onto the floor, 'we need to go.'

They went to the doorway and looked out into the empty corridor.

'Come on, let's move,' said Mickey.

They ran down the corridor to the side entrance. They poked their heads out. They could see the backs of some of the crowd who were watching the lion being lifted into the cage on the lorry.

'Let's get the bikes,' whispered Mickey.

They walked a few feet until they reached the bushes where their bikes were hidden. They then joined the back of the crowd while pushing their bikes. Then they both jumped.

'It's all very exciting isn't it?'

They turned round to see Mr Metcalfe standing behind them.

'It's amazing how word gets out so quickly,' he said as he looked around at the crowd. 'Anyway, don't let me stop you from getting a better view. Why don't you leave your bikes by those bushes and make your way to the front? You might be able to get quite close to the lion. You won't be able to look him in the eye exactly, but, well, anyway, don't be shy about going to the front.' Then he walked off.

'Been there, done that, got the T-shirt,' said Mickey.

'I've got to go,' said Charlie, as he looked at his watch. 'I've got twelve minutes. I'll see you tomorrow.'

'See you,' said Mickey.

Charlie worked his way around the edge of the crowd to the main gates. Then he got on his bike and set off, standing up on his pedals until he reached full speed.

He screeched to a halt in his driveway. He half threw his bike into the garage and then went through the backdoor into the kitchen. Charlie glanced at his watch. He had five seconds to spare.

'I'm glad you're safely home,' said his mother as he walked in. 'I nearly texted you. A lion had escaped from a crashed lorry on the way to the wildlife park. But I wasn't too worried. The lion went into the school and I knew you were with Mickey. If there's one place Mickey would not have gone it would have been the school.'

'We heard the police announcements on the loudspeaker,' said Charlie.

'But you kept away from the school?' said Mother.

'We saw the crowds gathering once it had been shot,' said Charlie. 'We went into the car park but couldn't get close at that point because there were so many people.'

'Did you see any teachers? It was supposed to be a parents' evening, wasn't it?'

'We saw Mr Metcalfe.'

'Poor Mr Metcalfe. Still, hopefully the lion didn't cause much damage. Would you like a squash?'

'Yes please,' said Charlie, who was relieved that the questioning had stopped. He hadn't lied and at least his mother now knew he had been there. After all, there may have been other parents who had seen him and might mention it to either his mother or father.

'Your dad's out in the garden,' said Mother. 'He's trimming the hedge. Reluctantly I might add. Gardening is not his favourite occupation.'

Charlie looked out the window and saw his father working his way along the hedge with the shears. Charlie thought of his idea he had had in the library. He knew his father would not be the best person to ask for help. His mother was right, he did not even like gardening, let alone know much about it.

Charlie went upstairs and lay on his bed and looked up at the space station hanging from the ceiling. The fact is, he didn't know much about gardening either. But maybe Emma and Geraldine did. He wondered what they would think of his idea. One thing was for sure, it would be a challenge.

– CHAPTER 9 –

The garden secret

Charlie bumped into Mickey as he walked through the main gates into school the following morning.

'What happened when you got home?' asked Charlie.

'I casually gave my mother the thruppence halfway through the evening,' said Mickey. 'She never realized it had gone missing.'

'No,' said Charlie, 'I mean, did she ask you where you had been? Does she know you went to the school and saw the lion?'

'No, mate. She didn't say anything about school. Anyway, what if she had?'

'She might have found out we had been inside the school,' said Charlie. 'If anybody finds out we will be in big trouble.'

'If I told my mother I had gone into the school and then gone into the school library she would never believe me anyway,' said Mickey.

'Yeah, well we must never tell anyone,' said Charlie.

'Keep your hair on,' said Mickey. 'Anyway, I don't know why you're so worried. It's not like anybody will be bothered that a lion was roaming round the school. Most people probably think he just went into the reception area and then walked straight out again.'

Then they heard Emma calling to them. She was sitting with Geraldine on the log in the natural play area.

'Have you heard about last night?' said Emma, as they reached them.

'What?' said Charlie, as he sat down.

'The lion of course,' said Emma. 'There was a lion roaming inside the school last night. They ended up having to cancel the parents' evening. Don't tell me you haven't heard about it. Everybody's talking about it.'

'What lion?' said Mickey, as he sat on the log.

'The lion that escaped,' said Emma. 'You must have heard. It was on the local news last night.'

'Oh, that lion,' said Mickey.

'Yes, THAT lion,' said Emma.

'He won't know anything about it,' said Geraldine. 'The only news he's interested in is football news.'

'That's not true,' said Mickey. 'I'm also interested in cricket news.'

'What about you Charlie?' said Emma. 'Surely you heard about it?'

'Yeah, I heard about it,' said Charlie.

'Well, at least show some enthusiasm,' said Emma as she puffed her cheeks and let out a big sigh. 'How can you both be so laid back about it?'

'It's no big deal,' said Mickey. 'It probably happens all the time in schools in the jungle.'

'Yes, but Heatherbridge is not in the jungle,' said Emma.

'I'll remember that next time we have a geography lesson,' said Mickey. 'I shall impress Mrs Drake with the interesting fact that Heatherbridge is not in the jungle.'

Then Rodney Spanner and another boy from Mr Daniel's class walked by. 'Hey, Dewhurst, I heard you were in the school last night.'

'Uh, what do you mean?' said Mickey.

Charlie held his breath.

'*What do you mean?*' said Rodney, imitating Mickey's voice. 'The lion that was in the school last night was probably him,' he said to the boy with him. 'After all, everybody mistook him for a lion at the wildlife park.'

Charlie let out a deep breath.

'But wait, the lion last night was a big, fierce, scary lion,' said Rodney. 'Not a little weedy one.' They both laughed and walked on.

'He is way out of order,' said Mickey.

'Just ignore him,' said Emma.

'Well I think what happened last night was terrible,' said Geraldine. 'Apparently, the lion went into the library. Why he would want to go in there I have no idea.'

'Me neither,' said Mickey. 'Why would anybody want to go into the library?'

'The point is, apparently he caused mayhem in there,' said Geraldine. 'The rumour is that the library will have to be closed all day while they clean it up.'

'It's not all bad news then,' said Mickey.

Charlie knew he had to try and change the subject before Mickey let out the secret of them being there. Then Charlie remembered his idea. 'By the way,' he said, 'I've come up with a good idea for Penny's great auntie.'

'A lion's just been ransacking the school and you want to talk about Penny's great auntie,' said Geraldine, shaking her head.

'What's your idea, Charlie?' asked Emma.

'Well, her garden is not in very good condition, is it? So I thought we could go and tidy it up and make it look better.'

'Charlie, that's a wonderful idea,' said Emma. 'Don't you agree, Geraldine?'

'It's got potential,' said Geraldine.

'Well, I think it's an excellent idea,' said Emma 'What made you think of it?'

But before Charlie had to answer, the bell rang. They all got up and walked into the school.

When they got back to the classroom from assembly they had to work on some maths. Mr Metcalfe had spoken about the lion in assembly and had even said he had seen some of the pupils in the car park. But much to Charlie's relief he had not mentioned any names.

They had been working for about half an hour when Mickey looked out the window. 'Woah, what's that doing here?'

Charlie looked up. The van from the local television channel had driven into the car park.

'They must be reporting about the lion,' said Geraldine.

'Anyway, how is the lion now?' asked Emma. 'Does anybody know?'

'I heard on the radio this morning that he was a bit groggy but he is going to be fine,' said Geraldine.

By now everybody had seen the van and were talking.

'Settle down everybody,' said Mrs Drake. 'It doesn't concern us directly.'

Then there was a knock at the door. The door opened and Mr Metcalfe walked in.

Charlie had an uneasy feeling. He looked at Mickey, but he did not seem worried.

'Mrs Drake I do apologize,' said Mr Metcalfe, 'but I wonder if I could have a word with everybody?'

'By all means,' said Mrs Drake.

'There's no problem,' said Mr Metcalfe. 'It's just that the television crew would like to do a live interview about the lion. I suggested that they might like to interview a pupil.' He looked over towards Charlie's table. 'Of course, I can't make anybody do it but …'

Geraldine put her hand up and had a beaming smile on her face. 'I don't mind doing the interview,' she said. 'I understand from a teacher who's been in the library that the lion left some scat on top of a book which was on the floor. I can talk about that and other things to do with tracking.'

'What's scat when it's at home?' said Mickey.

'It's the droppings left by a lion,' said Geraldine, shaking her head. 'Everybody knows that.'

Charlie looked around the class. He didn't reckon anybody else knew that fact.

Geraldine had put her hand down and was looking expectantly at Mr Metcalfe.

'Well, thank you for volunteering, Geraldine,' said Mr Metcalfe. 'But I thought as Charlie and Mickey were actually in the crowd in the car park when the lion was loaded onto the lorry that one of them might like to be interviewed.'

'You two were there?' said Geraldine. 'Why didn't you say?'

Charlie swallowed hard.

But Mickey had already put his hand up. 'I'll do the interview,' he said.

'Are you sure?' said Mr Metcalfe.

'Positive,' said Mickey.

'But you know nothing about lions,' said Geraldine.

'I do. I know all about scat for a start.'

'You had never heard of the word until a minute ago,' said Geraldine.

'I'm a fast learner,' said Mickey. 'Anyway, I know all about the place where they live. Don't forget, I've been there.'

'That was the enclosure at the Heatherbridge Wildlife Park,' said Geraldine, 'not the plains of Africa.'

'You need to come now if possible,' said Mr Metcalfe looking at his watch. 'Mrs Drake, will you excuse Mickey for a few minutes?'

'I suppose so,' said Mrs Drake, who didn't seem very happy.

'Are you crazy?' whispered Charlie as Mickey got up.

'It'll be a doddle,' muttered Mickey. 'I won't mention the library. Anyway, as long as it's not that same interviewer who interviewed me when the meteorite fell I will be fine.'

'Please hurry, Mickey,' said Mr Metcalfe. 'By the way, it's the same interviewer as when the meteorite fell, so he knows all about the school.'

By now Mickey was halfway to the front of the class. He looked back at Charlie, shrugged his shoulders and walked up to Mr Metcalfe.

'You might like to get the channel on the screen' said Mr Metcalfe to Mrs Drake. 'Then you can all watch the interview.' Then he and Mickey walked out.

'Very well,' said Mrs Drake, who sounded even less happy. 'Miss Rees will you please get the local TV channel on the screen.'

'This is going to be a disaster,' said Geraldine.

'Charlie, why didn't you say you and Mickey were in the car park last night?' said Emma.

'I didn't have chance.'

'Of course you did,' said Emma.

'You actually saw the lion?' said Geraldine.

'It was no big deal,' said Charlie.

'No big deal?' said Emma. 'You saw a lion in the school car park and it was no big deal?'

'Yeah, it was no big deal. There were loads of people there, not just us.'

Emma looked at him for what seemed like an age. Then she said, 'What's going on Charlie?'

'Nothing,' said Charlie.

But then the screen came to life. It was a lady speaking in the studio. 'The last we heard, Mr Bennet was recovering well in hospital. He said he would not be discouraged from trying again. He says he is determined to be the first person to walk backwards from Heatherbridge to Land's End. However, next time he will take somebody with him to warn him about bus stops and indeed other obstacles. And now back to our main story, Mason the Lion. We can go straight over to Rick who is live at Heatherbridge Junior School.'

Rick the reporter came on screen. 'Thank you, Charlotte. Yes, welcome to Heatherbridge Junior School where yesterday evening an escaped lion was shot with a tranquillizer in the school car park. I'm hoping to speak to one of the pupils in a moment. Mr Metcalfe the head teacher said he would bring out a volunteer.' He turned round. 'Ah here comes Mr Metcalfe now with …' But then he stopped speaking.

'Rick, are you alright?' Charlotte the presenter could be heard saying. 'Is there another lion?'

'No. I mean, yes I am fine,' said the reporter.

But Charlie didn't think he sounded fine at all.

'He's gone as white as a sheet,' said Geraldine. 'He's obviously remembered Mickey from last time.'

'Let me bring in this young man who witnessed the lion yesterday evening,' said the reporter. 'Good morning young man. I think we've met before, when the meteorite landed. It's Mickey isn't it?'

'Once seen never forgotten,' said Mickey, who then grinned at the camera.

'Perhaps you can tell us what you saw yesterday evening,' said the reporter.

'Well, it was a nice evening so I decided to go out for a bike ride. I headed to the park and waited ...'

'Perhaps we can skip that part,' said the reporter. 'Please tell the viewers what you saw in the car park.'

'Well, basically, they had shot the lion and he was out for the count on the tarmac. They then lifted him into a cage on the lorry using a tarpaulin.'

'Were you frightened?' asked the reporter.

'No, not all,' said Mickey.

Charlie thought Mickey was doing well. He knew as long as the library wasn't mentioned there wouldn't be a problem. Then the reporter mentioned the library.

'The headteacher tells me the lion has caused some damage in the library,' said the reporter.

'Yes, apparently,' said Mickey. 'There was a big dollop of scat on a book.'

'Let's hope the book wasn't important,' said the reporter.

'It wasn't,' said Mickey. 'It was just a book on advanced maths.'

'I see,' said the reporter.

'How does he know that?' said Geraldine.

'You said yourself it landed on a book,' said Emma.

'Yes, but I never mentioned what the book was about.'

Meanwhile, the reporter was talking to Mickey. 'Well young man, I expect you never expected to see a lion in your school car park.'

'No,' said Mickey. 'Giraffes possibly, tigers maybe, but a lion – I for one, Rick, am in total shock.' For a couple of seconds he stared unblinking at the reporter with a serious look on his face. Then he turned to the camera and winked.

'This is embarrassing,' said Geraldine.

'Well, that's the latest on the lion at Heatherbridge Junior School,' said the reporter. 'I've certainly had the lion's share of the reporting today. Now, back to you Charlotte.'

But as the screen switched back to the presenter in the studio Mickey could be heard saying, 'That was a terrible joke.'

At break time Charlie went out and sat on the log. He had hardly spoken to Mickey since he had come back into the classroom. Then he looked up and saw Mickey walking up to him.

'What's up?' said Mickey.

'You blew it,' said Charlie.

'What do you mean?' said Mickey.

'You blew it. You said the book was about advanced maths. The only way you could know that was if you were there.'

'Not necessarily,' said Mickey. 'Anyway, Mr Metcalfe didn't notice. He seemed happy enough. At least, he was happier than Rick the Reporter. Not that that takes much.'

Charlie shook his head and said nothing.

'Speaking of happy people,' said Mickey, 'here come some now. I'm off to play football.'

Charlie looked up and saw Emma, Geraldine and Penny coming toward him. They all three sat on the log.

Nobody said anything for a while and then Emma spoke.

'I've mentioned your idea to Penny and she thinks it's a good idea too. Isn't that right, Penny?'

'Yes, but we can't just turn up there. We could go to see her this evening and make some arrangements.'

'Are you free, Geraldine?' asked Emma.

'Just for a short while, I suppose,' she said.

'How about you Charlie?' asked Emma.

'I guess so. But I don't know much about gardening.'

They sat in silence for a while.

Then Emma said, 'Charlie, what happened last night?'

'It's a secret really,' said Charlie.

'Charlie,' said Geraldine, 'how did Mickey know that book was an advanced maths book?'

'And why,' said Emma, 'didn't you tell us you had been in the school car park last night? In fact, why were you anywhere near here last night?'

Charlie thought for a moment then said, 'What I'm going to tell you is top secret, okay?'

They all nodded.

Charlie took a deep breath and told them everything.

'So that's why all the books had been thrown out of the spaces under the seats,' said Geraldine, when Charlie had finished his story. 'I heard two of the teachers saying they couldn't understand how the lion had got them all out.'

'And this book that gave you the garden idea,' said Emma, 'do you think we can find it again? It might come in useful.'

'Yeah. It's probably just been put back in the storage space.'

'Well, our next job is to find it and see if we can borrow it,' said Emma.

'I heard the library's going to be open at lunchtime so we can get it then,' said Geraldine.

'But no one must ever know what happened and why we know about the book,' said Charlie.

'Don't worry about it,' said Emma. 'You've heard of the secret garden? Well, this is the garden secret.'

– CHAPTER 10 –

The garden plan

'Right,' said Emma, as they finished their sandwiches at lunchtime, 'we need to go to the library.'

'You mean to find the book on gardening?' said Geraldine.

'If we can,' said Emma. 'Is the library definitely open now?'

'As far as I know,' said Geraldine.

'Are you two coming?' said Emma.

Charlie and Mickey looked at each other.

'I guess so,' said Charlie.

Mickey shrugged. 'I suppose I had better come. I might have to protect you all from a charging lion like I protected Charlie last night.'

'Yeah, right,' said Charlie, as they all got up. 'I don't think hiding in a box and whimpering, *nice little lion*, provided much protection.'

'I was cleverly drawing his attention away from you,' said Mickey.

'Look, there's Penny,' said Emma.

Penny was walking out of the hall.

'Penny,' said Emma, 'we're just going to the library to see if we can find that book that Charlie saw. It might give us some tips for your auntie's garden. Do you wanna come too?'

'Okay,' said Penny as she tagged along.

'Why did you have to go and tell them everything?' said Mickey to Charlie, as they followed the others. 'I thought it was supposed to be a big secret.'

'For a start I had to try and explain why you knew the lion had done the you-know-what on an advanced maths book,' said Charlie. 'You shouldn't have said that on TV.'

'I was under pressure from the world's press,' said Mickey.

'The local news channel is hardly the world's press,' said Geraldine.

'This is supposed to be a private conversation between me and Charlie,' said Mickey.

'You're not very good at keeping things private are you?' said Geraldine.

'Not when I'm speaking to the world's press,' said Mickey.

But then they reached the library.

Charlie looked around as they walked in. Everything had been cleaned up and there was no sign that a lion had been in there the previous evening.

'So which seat space was that book in Charlie?' said Emma.

'That one there,' said Charlie, pointing. 'Mickey was in that one next to it.'

'Well let's have a look through both of them while nobody else is here,' said Emma.

Emma lifted the seat Charlie had been in and Geraldine lifted the seat next to it.

'Charlie, what were the reference details?' said Geraldine.

'What do you mean?' said Charlie.

'The reference details for the book, Charlie.'

Charlie still didn't understand.

'Come on, it's obvious, Charlie,' said Mickey.

'What does she mean, then?' said Charlie, feeling embarrassed.

'I haven't got a clue, mate,' said Mickey.

'So much for being obvious,' said Charlie.

'Charlie, what was the book called?' said Geraldine. 'And who was the author, what year was it published, who was the publisher and where was it published?'

'Don't be silly, Geraldine,' said Emma. 'Charlie, what was the book called?'

'Something like, 'Make Your Grandparent's Garden Great – Gardening Tips for Grandkids.''

'Thank you, Charlie,' said Emma.

Charlie, Emma and Penny began rummaging through the books in the seat Charlie had hidden in. Geraldine and Mickey were looking in the other seat.

'I don't think all the books have been put back in here,' said Mickey, as he and Geraldine searched through the books. 'There's just about room enough for me to get in here without taking books out.'

'I don't think so,' said Geraldine.

'There is,' said Mickey. 'I'll prove it.' He dived into the box, lay on top of the books and pulled the seat down. 'Told you I could,' said a muffled voice.

'Don't be so childish,' said Geraldine.

And that's when they heard the voice of Mr Metcalfe in the corridor.

'Mrs Harcourt, allow me to show you the library,' he said as he walked in, looking back to a lady who was following him.

Emma put the seat down where she, Charlie and Penny had been searching. Geraldine calmly took hold of a nearby book and sat down on her seat.

Charlie thought he heard a muffled 'help' coming from inside her seat.

'Ah, these are some of Mrs Drake's class,' said Mr Metcalfe. 'Children, this is Mrs Harcourt who is one of our new governors. I'm just showing her around the school.'

'Good afternoon, children,' said Mrs Harcourt.

'Good afternoon, Mrs Harcourt,' they said, including Geraldine who had now stood up.

'I must say it's good to see you making use of what is clearly a wonderful library,' said Mrs Harcourt.

'Yes, we like to think that our library is one of the jewels in our crown so to speak,' said Mr Metcalfe.

'Now, is not this where the lion came last night?' she said.

'Yes, he made rather a mess but it has all been tidied up,' said Mr Metcalfe.

'I watched your pupil being interviewed on the TV this morning. Mickey isn't?'

'Yes, Mickey,' said Mr Metcalfe, with a sigh.

'He seemed very confident,' said Mrs Harcourt. 'And I was impressed that he even knew that there is such a thing as an advanced maths book. His little throwaway remark that it wasn't important was quite amusing. One got the impression he was really very good at maths. I suppose if you are beyond the advanced stage then it would not seem very important. You must be very proud to have such a unique student in your school, Mr Metcalfe.'

'Well, yes, he is certainly unique,' said Mr Metcalfe. 'But then all our students are unique.'

'Tactfully put Mr Metcalfe, but not every student could talk about advanced maths on TV. Is he in your class, children?'

'He shares a table with Charlie, Geraldine and Emma,' said Mr Metcalfe, as he pointed to each in turn.

'Well, let's hope some of his undoubted star quality rubs off on the rest of you,' said Mrs Harcourt.

Charlie glanced at Geraldine. She looked furious.

'I'm surprised he's not in the library now,' said Mrs Harcourt, as she surveyed the room. 'You would think he would be taking every opportunity to increase his knowledge.'

'I think we must be getting on,' said Mr Metcalfe, looking at his watch.

They both turned to walk out.

That's when the sound of somebody sneezing came from inside the seat by Geraldine.

They both stopped.

'Did I hear a noise coming from inside that seat?' said Mrs Harcourt. 'Or were my ears deceiving me?'

Mr Metcalfe looked puzzled for a moment, then he seemed to realize who was in the seat. Now he looked worried. 'Uh, what noise, Mrs Harcourt?'

'I distinctly heard the sound of somebody sneezing coming from inside that seat.'

'Perhaps it was a lion,' said Mr Metcalfe, with a weak smile. 'It will be the end of lunch, soon,' he said, looking at his watch again. 'We need to proceed with your guided tour.'

'Mr Metcalfe, I definitely heard the sound of sneezing. There is somebody inside that seat.' She stood there pointing at it. 'I think you should have a look.'

'Very well,' said Mr Metcalfe. He sighed and started to walk towards the seat.

Charlie, who was right by the seat, thought he heard the words, *oh that's just great*, coming from inside the seat. Then he thought he heard the sound of the rustling of books.

By now, Mr Metcalfe had reached the seat. He lifted it up and they all looked inside.

Mickey was lying on his back, his face hidden by a book he was holding and apparently reading.

'Mickey Dewhurst, what are you doing?' said Mr Metcalfe.

He moved the book away from his face. 'I am trying to take every opportunity to increase my knowledge,' he said. 'This is the only place I can read without being disturbed - until now.'

Mrs Harcourt bent down, picked up the book he had been reading, and read out its title. 'Make Your Grandparent's Garden Great – Top Tips for Gardening Grandkids'.

'I don't know much about gardening so I thought I should learn more,' said Mickey, who by now had put his hands behind his head.

'Well, you are setting a good example by not just studying intellectual topics like advanced maths,' said Mrs Harcourt. 'But your method of study is unusual. It must be very dark in there. You could strain your eyes. But as you say, you must not be disturbed when studying.'

'Mickey Dewhurst, get out,' said Mr Metcalfe. 'There is more opportunity to increase your knowledge out here than in there.'

Mickey clambered out.

'Here is your book, young man,' said Mrs Harcourt as she gave it him back. She looked at him for a moment. 'Mr Metcalfe is right, you are certainly unique.'

Mr Metcalfe shook his head. 'We really must be going,' he said.

'Goodbye everybody,' said Mrs Harcourt.

Then they both walked out

'That was majorly embarrassing,' said Mickey. 'If I hadn't sneezed I would have got away with it. Still, at least I've got star quality.'

'The whole thing was an embarrassment,' said Geraldine. 'You've made the school look ridiculous – yet again.'

'The bell will be going soon,' said Emma. 'We need to make arrangements.'

'I shall take this book out and look at it at home,' said Geraldine, as she took it off Mickey.

'So much for me increasing my knowledge,' he said.

'Look, can we all agree to meet at the park at seven o'clock?' said Emma. 'Then we can all go to Penny's auntie to tell her about the idea.'

They all nodded in agreement, except Mickey.

'Mickey, are you going to come too?' said Emma.

'Count me out. It's not exactly my thing.'

'Well, at least come tomorrow,' said Emma. 'We will need you to help with the gardening.'

'He knows nothing about gardening,' said Geraldine.

'I do,' said Mickey, 'but I just don't fancy spending Saturday morning pulling out weeds and planting tulips.'

'It's not just fiddly stuff,' said Emma. 'For a start the old bit of lawn will need digging up.'

'Count me out,' said Mickey.

'If you change your mind you'll be most welcome,' said Penny. 'She lives at Twenty-three Linnell Road.'

Then the bell went for end of the lunch break.

'Well, it will certainly be a challenge,' said Father, as they finished dinner.

'Are you sure Penny's auntie wants you to dig in her garden?' said Mother.

'I think so,' said Charlie. 'Anyway, we will see her tonight.'

'What about tools?' said Father. 'Do you want to take our spade?'

'She's got loads of tools in her shed I think,' said Charlie.

'You had better get going Charlie if you've got to be at the park by seven,' said Mother. 'Make sure you're back by eight, okay?'

'Thanks Mum,' said Charlie. He dashed out to get his bike and he was soon on his way.

'Well, this is a nice surprise,' said Auntie Edith as the four of them walked into the back garden. 'To what do I owe this pleasure?'

'We've had an idea,' said Penny. 'Well, it was Charlie's idea really.'

'An idea, what do you mean?'

'It's to do with your garden,' said Penny.

'Well, let me get my folding chair and you all squeeze onto that old bench and you can tell me all about it.'

They sat on the bench and Auntie Edith fetched her chair which was leaning against the wall of the house. She brought it over, walking gingerly over the broken patio stones, unfolded it and sat down. 'Now then,' she said, 'tell me about your idea.'

'We wanted to do something for you after you had explained to us about the time capsule,' said Penny.

'And you went to the trouble of putting it together in the first place,' said Emma.

'That was a long time ago, my dear. And it was a pleasure to talk to you about it. You really don't need to do anything for me.'

'We couldn't think what to do or get you,' said Penny. 'Then Charlie had an idea.'

Penny stopped speaking and everybody turned to Charlie. He felt embarrassed and was quite happy for the others to do the talking.

'You tell Auntie Edith, Charlie,' said Penny. 'Tell her about your idea.'

'Well,' said Charlie. 'I thought we could do some gardening for you and make your garden tidier.'

'That's a wonderful idea,' said Auntie Edith. 'What made you come up with such a good idea?'

Charlie coughed and wasn't sure what to say.

'He came across a book in our school library,' said Geraldine. 'It's written for children and is about looking after the gardens of elderly relatives.'

'Well, I don't know what to say I'm sure,' said Auntie Edith.

'Would you like us to do some gardening?' said Penny.

'Penny, my dear, I would be delighted. But there is a lot to do. I don't expect you will be able to make much difference.'

'I've started looking at the book,' said Geraldine. 'I'll have a few ideas by tomorrow.'

'Tomorrow?' said Auntie Edith. 'So soon?'

'Will that be alright?' said Penny.

'Of course it will,' said Auntie Edith. 'I am not an early riser. But you are welcome to come and start working before I am up. The shed isn't locked and it has plenty of spades and forks and such like.'

'I propose we start early,' said Geraldine. 'Let's try and get here by half-past eight.'

They all nodded in agreement.

'Auntie Edith, is there anything particular you want us to leave in the garden?' asked Penny.

'There is nothing sentimental there anymore,' she said. 'It's mostly weeds. So you can do whatever you like. And this bit of lawn is well past its prime. It needs replacing. But of course you won't be able to do that.'

'Perhaps we should have a quick look around,' said Geraldine.

'By all means,' she said and she pushed herself up from the chair.

They all got up and began making their way through the undergrowth.

Then Auntie Edith stopped and waved to a man a few gardens down. 'Hello,' she shouted.

The man waved back.

Charlie thought he recognized him.

'That's the manager of Heatherbridge supermarket,' said Auntie Edith. 'He lives at number thirty-three.'

'This garden certainly needs a lot doing to it,' said Geraldine, who had walked further down.

'It certainly does,' said Auntie Edith. 'But if you can do anything to make it tidier I would be most grateful.'

As Charlie looked around the garden he saw it was in an even worse condition than he had realized. His father was right, he thought, it would definitely be a challenge.

– CHAPTER 11 –

The garden challenge

Charlie glanced at his watch as he cycled towards Linnell Road on Saturday morning. It was 8.25. He should get there on time. He was probably cycling too fast. But he had heard some good news. The garden challenge had just got a little easier. Then up ahead he saw Emma, Geraldine, and Penny.

'Hi there!' he shouted.

They stopped cycling and waited for him.

'Hi Charlie,' said Emma, as he caught up.

'I've got good news,' said Charlie.

'What?' said Geraldine.

He got his phone out, switched it on and held it up. 'I got this text from Mickey this morning.'

Geraldine took the phone off him and read the message out loud. 'Count me in. What time?'

'Count him in for what?' said Penny.

'I presume he means he's coming to help,' said Geraldine.

'That's brilliant!' said Emma.

'If you say so,' said Geraldine.

'Of course it is,' said Emma. 'We can use all the help we can get.'

'Let's hope he will be a help and not a hindrance,' said Geraldine.

'Don't be so horrible,' said Emma. 'I knew he would come in the end. Now we can really make a difference in Auntie Edith's garden.'

'Did you text him back?' said Geraldine, as she handed the phone back to Charlie.

'Yeah, I said 8.30.'

Then Charlie's phone rang.

'Hello?' said Charlie.

'It's me,' said Mickey. 'I've arrived. I wandered around the back but you're not here.'

'It's not 8.30 yet,' said Charlie, as he glanced at his watch. 'It's only 8.29.'

'Very funny,' said Mickey.

'We're all here near Linnell Road,' said Charlie. 'We'll be there in a minute.'

'Okay. I'll go to the shed, get a spade and start digging up the lawn. You did say she wants the lawn digging up?'

'Yeah,' said Charlie. 'Hang on, Emma's saying something.'

'Charlie, tell him not to knock on the door and to be quiet. Penny's auntie might still be sleeping.'

'Did you get that?' said Charlie.

'Tell her I shall be like a Ninja,' said Mickey, who then rang off.

'He says he will be like a Ninja,' said Charlie.

'What's he on about?' said Emma.

'The Ninja were covert agents in Japan around the fifteenth century,' said Geraldine. 'They were meant to be good at moving silently and with stealth. Later legends said they could become invisible so you wouldn't know they were there. In other words, they were completely the opposite to Mickey.'

'Well I think it's really good that he's joining in,' said Emma.

'And he's started before us,' said Penny.

'Yeah, and we're now late,' said Charlie as he looked at his watch.

'Come on, let's get going,' said Emma.

They got on their bikes and soon reached the drive of Auntie Edith's house.

Emma put her finger up to her mouth to remind them to be quiet.

They got off their bikes and wheeled them around to the back of the house.

When they got there they all stood in silence, looking at the garden.

'Where is he?' said Geraldine.

'I dunno,' said Charlie.

'I can't even see his bike,' said Penny.

'Charlie, give him a ring to find out what he's doing,' said Emma.

Charlie got his phone out and waited for Mickey to answer.

'Hello?' said Mickey. 'Where are you all?'

'We're here,' said Charlie. 'Where are you?'

'I'm here,' said Mickey.

'What do you mean *here*?'

'I'm here at Auntie what's her name's place.'

'Are you sure?' said Charlie.

'Of course I'm sure. Thirty-three Linnell Road. I double-checked when I came in. This house is definitely thirty-three. By the way, I'm no gardening expert but this lawn doesn't look too bad. Still, we aim to please.'

'There he is,' said Penny.

They looked across the gardens.

'That's him in the high visibility jacket,' said Penny.

'So much for being a ninja,' said Geraldine.

'Mickey,' said Charlie, 'you're at the …'

But then they heard a man shouting. 'What are you doing?'

They saw Mickey jump and drop his phone.

'He says he's at number thirty-three,' said Charlie, turning to the others.

'That's the supermarket manager's house,' said Emma.

Mickey's phone was still on and he had not picked it up. Charlie put his phone on loudspeaker and they all listened.

'What are you doing?' said the supermarket manager again.

'I'm about to start digging up the lawn,' said Mickey. 'Have you come to help? Or are you just making deliveries?'

'No, I am not making deliveries. Supermarket managers do not make deliveries.'

'Okay, well grab a spade from the shed and give us a hand,' said Mickey.

'Why would I want to dig up my own lawn?'

'Don't ask me, ask Auntie what's her … uh, what do you mean, *my lawn*?'

'My lawn. Why would I want to dig up my own lawn?'

They saw Mickey stare at the supermarket manager. Then he turned slowly and looked across the gardens.

Emma raised her hand and gave him a wave.

Mickey sort of waved back.

'Well?' said the supermarket manager.

'I think I might be at the wrong house,' said Mickey.

'Let me be a bit more definite,' said the supermarket manager. 'You ARE at the wrong house. I think you'll find your friends are at number twenty-three.'

'I'll just put the spade back in the shed,' said Mickey.

'Leave it where it is,' said the manager. 'Just get out.'

'I can trim the edge of your lawn before I go if you …'

'Out,' said the manager, pointing.

'That's a bit off,' said Mickey. 'I offer to trim your lawn and now you're going to turf me out. That's a gardening joke by the way.'

'Out,' said the manager. 'Out, out, out!'

'Have you ever thought of being a cricket umpire?' said Mickey.

The manager said nothing but stood there pointing.

Mickey picked up his phone, went to his bike and walked out.

'Unbelievable,' said Geraldine.

'It's an easy mistake to make,' said Emma.

'He certainly made it look easy,' said Geraldine. 'Anyway, we had better start deciding what to do.' She took off her backpack, opened it up and lifted out the book on gardening.

'This garden looks a bit daunting,' said Emma, as Geraldine started looking through the book.

'You're right,' said Penny. 'I think we may have bitten off more than we can chew.'

'We just need to get going,' said Charlie, who was feeling impatient.

'Okay, here we are,' said Geraldine, as she turned over a page in the book. *'Where to start with overgrown gardens.* Right, it says the first thing we must do is clear the garden of any litter or other rubbish, such as bits of wood or broken pottery.'

'Morning everybody. Are you sure this is the right house?'

They turned round. It was Mickey.

'Of course it's the right house,' said Geraldine.

'Okay, okay, I just thought I would check. You can't be too careful.'

'Geraldine is just explaining what we need to do first,' said Emma.

'Since when has she been the boss?' said Mickey, as he took off his jacket and threw it to one side.

'Now,' said Geraldine, 'we need to get something to put all the rubbish in.'

'That looks like a couple of plastic tubs sticking out from behind the shed,' said Emma. 'They're the ones with handles.'

'Excellent,' said Geraldine. 'I'll grab them and you four space yourselves across the bottom of the garden. Then we'll slowly walk back, picking anything up as we go.'

They walked down to the bottom of the garden. Emma walked over to far left. Then there was Penny, then Charlie, with Mickey on the right.

Geraldine carried the tubs over and put one a couple of yards in front of Penny and the other in front of Charlie. 'Okay everybody. Start walking slowly back down the garden and throw any rubbish you come across into the nearest bin.'

They started walking. Charlie soon found an old sweet wrapper and then some broken pieces of bamboo.

'This looks like a piece of a saucer,' said Emma, as she threw a piece of pottery into a tub.

'What's this when it's at home?' said Mickey. He held up a grubby piece of knitted wool.

'That looks like one of my old mittens,' said Penny. 'I probably lost it when I was playing in Auntie Edith's garden when I was younger.'

'It's so exciting,' said Emma. 'It's like a treasure hunt.'

'I wouldn't call an old mitten treasure,' said Mickey. 'And I wouldn't call this exciting.'

'Stop moaning and keep going,' said Geraldine as she pulled one of the tubs a few feet further up the garden.

'Anyway, why aren't you picking up anything?' said Mickey.

'I'm co-ordinating and I am in charge of moving the tubs,' said Geraldine.

'Nice work if you can get it,' said Mickey.

'Just keep working your way up the garden, everybody,' said Geraldine.

'Slavedriver,' said Mickey.

After ten minutes they reached the patio.

'Well done everybody,' said Geraldine. 'We've nearly filled two tubs with rubbish.'

'The garden's looking better already,' said Emma. 'What do you reckon, Charlie?'

'I guess so,' he said, as he looked back down the garden, although he didn't think it looked that much different with all the weeds still there.

'Well, well, well. You HAVE been working hard.'

They turned round to see Auntie Edith at the backdoor.

'Hello, Auntie Edith,' said Penny. 'We've collected nearly two tubs of rubbish.'

'Well I never,' said Auntie Edith. 'Who would have thought so much rubbish could be found in so small a garden.'

'I collected most of it,' said Mickey.

'Ah, now we haven't met before have we?' said Auntie Edith. 'You must be Mickey, the discoverer of the time capsule.'

'That's me,' said Mickey.

'Well, thank you for finding it and thank you for coming to help in my garden.'

'It's what I do,' said Mickey.

'We really must be getting on,' said Geraldine, shaking her head as she looked at Mickey.

'I see you have come prepared with a book,' said Auntie Edith to Geraldine. 'What is the next thing it tells you to do?'

'We have to get the weeds out now,' said Geraldine.

'Ah, now I might be able to help you there,' said Auntie Edith. 'If you look in the shed you should find large garden waste bags. You can put the weeds in those.'

'That will be most helpful,' said Geraldine.

'I'll go and get them,' said Emma. She walked off towards the shed.

'What do you want me to do?' asked Mickey. 'Shall I start digging up the lawn?'

'No, we need to concentrate on the weeding,' said Geraldine.

'Great,' said Mickey.

'Now then, this must be thirsty work,' said Auntie Edith. 'How would you all like some homemade lemonade?'

'Yes please, Auntie Edith,' said Penny. 'Your homemade lemonade is the best ever.'

'I'm not sure about that,' said Auntie Edith, laughing. 'I shall return presently.' She disappeared back inside the house.

'What are we going to do with all the rubbish and weeds?' said Emma, as she returned from the shed carrying the bags.

'When we go home for lunch I'll ask my dad if he can come round with the car this afternoon and take it all to the tip,' said Geraldine. 'Right, let's start pulling weeds out. Emma and Penny, you work on the left of that path. Charlie and Mickey work on the right.'

'What are you going to do?' asked Mickey.

'I'm busy carrying the burden of leadership,' said Geraldine. 'Now, it says in this book that you must pull weeds up by their roots. If you just break them off and leave the roots in the ground they will just grow back even more. So make sure you all pull everything out by the roots. Okay, let's get going.'

They all went back down the garden and started pulling up the weeds.

Then they heard Auntie Edith calling out. 'Homemade lemonade everybody.'

They walked over to the patio where Auntie Edith was standing with a tray loaded with glasses of lemonade.

'Woah,' said Mickey as he stumbled on the patio. 'These slabs are way off.'

'Yes, you need to be careful,' said Auntie Edith. 'This patio needs re-laying.'

'This lemonade is the best,' said Penny.

'I agree,' said Emma.

'Okay, everybody,' said Geraldine as she gulped down the last of her drink. 'Everybody back to work.'

'Like I said, you're a slavedriver,' said Mickey.

They put their glasses on the tray, thanked Auntie Edith and went back down the garden.

After about half hour Emma said: 'Our bag is full, I'll take it up to the top of the garden.'

'Okay,' said Penny.

Charlie straightened his back and watched Emma carrying the bag. Then he bent back down to carry on weeding. Then he heard a scream.

'What's wrong, Emma?' shouted Penny.

Emma was half-sitting, half-lying on the patio.

They all ran up to her.

'What happened?' said Penny.

'I twisted my ankle. I trod awkwardly on the edge of a slab.'

'I tried to warn everybody,' said Mickey.

'Mickey, be quiet,' said Geraldine. 'Emma, which ankle is it?'

'The right one,' said Emma, as she rubbed it. She started to cry.

'Let's see if you can stand up. Penny, you get that side and I'll stay this side. Let's help her up.'

They put their arms under her armpits and lifted her up. She stood on her left leg with her right foot in the air.

'Okay, try putting your right foot on the ground,' said Geraldine. 'Let's see if you can weight-bear.'

She put her foot down onto the ground. At first, she seemed okay.

'Are you putting any weight on it?' said Geraldine.

'Not really,' said Emma, as she lifted her foot up again.

'Well, give it a go,' said Geraldine.

Emma put her put foot down, but this time she cried out.
'Let me sit,' she said.

They lowered her back down to the ground.

'I think this could be a serious injury,' said Geraldine.

– CHAPTER 12 –

With a little help

As Emma sat on the floor crying and rubbing her ankle Penny went indoors to get Auntie Edith.

'Oh, my poor child,' said Auntie Edith as she walked onto the patio. 'I knew I should have got these slabs re-laid.'

'It's not your fault,' said Emma, as she sniffled and blew her nose on a handkerchief.

'Now, it's a pity one of us is not a first aider,' said Auntie Edith.

'There is a first-aider here,' said Mickey.

'You're a first-aider?' said Auntie Edith.

'Nope, not me.'

'Which of you is a first-aider then?' asked Auntie Edith. Mickey pointed to Emma.

'You're a first aider young lady?' said Auntie Edith.

'Yes,' said Emma, as she wiped her nose again.

'That's a fine how-do-you-do,' said Auntie Edith. 'The first-aider is the person who needs first aid.'

'Rice,' said Emma. 'I need rice. It stands for rest, ice, compression, and elevation. That's what you do for sprained or broken ankles.'

'Well, I can get some ice from the freezer,' said Auntie Edith. 'And I presume by compression you mean a bandage?'

'Yes,' said Emma.

'I shall go and get some ice and I'm sure I have a bandage somewhere,' said Auntie Edith. 'While I do that, you four can get poor Emma onto a chair and elevate her ankle using an upturned bucket or such like. And once you're settled on the chair, young lady, I suggest you give your parents a phone call to let them know what has happened. What they will think I do not know.' She shook her head and walked back into the house.

'Come on let's use that chair over there,' said Geraldine. 'Give us a hand, Penny.'

They lifted Emma up with their arms under her armpits. They then walked her over to the chair although she really hopped most of the way.

'Grab that bucket over there, Mickey,' said Geraldine.

'Yes, boss,' said Mickey. He walked over to it and picked it up. 'Right, I've grabbed hold of it,' he said. 'What do you want me to do with it now?'

'Mickey, stop being so childish and bring it over here,' said Geraldine.

'Just trying to bring some humour to the proceedings.'

'You're trying that's for sure,' said Geraldine as she snatched the bucket off Mickey, turned it upside down and placed it under Emma's foot.

'How does that feel Em?' said Charlie

'Okay, thanks, Charlie,' said Emma.

'You know Charlie, it's a shame it wasn't you who twisted your right ankle,' said Mickey. 'Then all we'd need to do was stick your artificial leg in a vice and straighten it.'

'Mickey, what is your problem?' said Geraldine.

'Well, it's true, isn't it Charlie?' said Mickey.

'I s'pose so.'

'Don't be horrible, Mickey,' said Emma.

'See Mickey, now you've upset Emma,' said Geraldine.

'My humour is wasted round here,' said Mickey.

'Emma, have you got your phone?' asked Geraldine.

'Yes, it's here,' she said as she took it out of her pocket.

'Okay, give your parents a ring,' said Geraldine.

'Penny, can you take this ice off me, please?' Charlie turned round to see Auntie Edith walking out.

'I've put the ice in this sealed plastic bag,' she said.

Penny took it off her and placed it against Emma's ankle.

'Now, here is some bandage you can use,' said Auntie Edith.

Geraldine took it off her and wrapped it around the ankle. 'I won't wrap it round the bag as well,' she said. 'I'll rest the bag against the bandage once the bandage is on. Am I doing it right, Emma?'

'Yes, it's fine, thank you,' she said as she tapped the front of her phone and then held it to her ear. Within seconds her call was answered. 'Hi Mum, I've had an accident,' she said.

For the second time that day Charlie cycled towards Auntie Edith's house in Linnell Road. It was after lunch and the four of them had agreed to carry on in the garden despite Emma not being there. When her mother had collected her she said she would take her straight to the Accident and Emergency Department in the hospital.

'Make sure you finish the garden,' were Emma's last words before she hobbled out of sight supported by her mother.

But Charlie was beginning to regret taking on the challenge of the garden. They had tidied it a little and got some weeds up, but he didn't think they had made that much difference. His mother had said she would see what she could do to help. But she said she wouldn't be able to spend any time there as she had to visit his grandpa. So he didn't think she would be able to do much.

As he approached Linnell road he heard his name being called.

'Charlie!'

He turned round to see Geraldine cycling towards him. He stopped and waited for her to catch up.

'Any news about Emma?' said Geraldine.

'I haven't heard anything. She's probably still waiting to be seen.'

'Anyway, we should be able to get some more done this afternoon,' said Geraldine.

'I guess so,' said Charlie.

'You don't sound convinced. Anyway, we'd better get going.' She set off cycling along the path.

Charlie got on his bike again and cycled after her. She's right, he thought, he was not convinced.

They got to Linnell Road and rode down towards Auntie Edith's house. Then they both stopped.

'What is going on down there?' asked Geraldine. 'What's that lorry for?'

'I dunno,' said Charlie. 'It's probably nothing to do with Penny's auntie.'

'Of course it is,' said Geraldine. 'It's parked up on the kerb right by her house and there's a man wearing a cap carrying something from the lorry down her driveway.'

'I recognize him,' said Charlie. 'It's Mickey's dad.'

Then they saw Mickey appear from the driveway and take something off the lorry and walk back towards the house.

'What is he doing?' said Geraldine.

They both started cycling again and soon reached Auntie Edith's house. As they arrived, Mickey was walking back up the driveway.

'What's going on?' asked Charlie.

'It's my dad,' said Mickey. 'He works at the quarry and he was doing a half day there this morning. I phoned him and told him about the patio. So he's brought a few offcuts they don't want and he reckons what with them and the slabs already there he should be able to get it levelled in an hour or so.'

'Mickey, you are not totally useless after all,' said Geraldine.

'Coming from you that's high praise,' said Mickey, who sounded quite pleased with himself.

Charlie and Geraldine pushed their bikes round to the back of the house.

'Afternoon all,' said Mr Dewhurst, who was busy lifting a slab up from the patio. 'We'll soon have this patio fixed in no time. And that Auntie Edith is making me a brew so it's all good.'

'Here's your mug of tea,' said Auntie Edith as she walked out from the kitchen.

'Ah, thank thee kindly,' said Mr Dewhurst. 'You can't beat a good brew. I'll tell thee that f'nowt.'

'I must say it's very kind of you to help,' said Auntie Edith.

'No problem at all,' he said. 'We'll have this patio as level as a bowling green in no time.'

'Speaking of bowling greens,' said Geraldine, 'when I asked my dad about collecting the rubbish and told him about the lawn he reckoned he might be able to save it. He said he would look at it when he came.'

'Well, I'm not sure about that,' said Auntie Edith. 'But he is very welcome to have a look at it.'

'Here's another piece of paving, Dad'. Mickey staggered over the still-bumpy patio and dropped it on some sandy soil where his father had removed some slabs.

'That's grand lad.' 'Right,' he said, as he put his mug down on the window ledge, 'you lot leave me alone while I sort out this 'ere patio. Mickey, you can return to your natural habitat and pull out some of those weeds over there.'

'Great,' said Mickey. He trudged off down the garden.

Then Penny walked out from the house. 'I've finished the drying up, Auntie Edith.'

'Thank you, my dear,' said Auntie Edith.

'How am I supposed to level this patio to the required standard with everybody standing on it?' said Mr Dewhurst. He lifted his cap off his head and put it back on again with a huff.

Auntie Edith grinned at everybody and walked back into the house. Everybody else went down the garden to join Mickey.

They all carried on weeding but then Geraldine stopped and went over to her backpack by the shed.

'Look out, we're about to get our next set of instructions from the boss,' said Mickey.

'Right,' said Geraldine. 'Now we've got rid of a lot of the weeds, we need to think about digging over the garden. Charlie and Mickey, get a couple of spades from the shed and start digging the patches where you've been weeding.'

They went over to the shed and each got a spade.

'And when you're digging, pull out any more weeds or roots of weeds you come across,' said Geraldine.

'I tell you, Charlie,' said Mickey, as he started digging, 'she's a slavedriver.'

Charlie looked at the large patch he had to dig. 'Maybe you're right,' he said. Then he took a deep breath, and he too started digging.

Nobody said anything for a while as they dug and weeded. After a while Charlie realized he had done most of his patch. But what were they supposed to do with it now? It was then that he heard his mother call out.

She was standing at the top of the garden and was holding something.

Charlie walked up to see her being careful to keep well out of the way of Mr Dewhurst, who was on his hands and knees positioning a new piece of slab.

'Hi, Charlie,' said his mother. 'I've been to the garden centre and bought these.' She was holding a wooden tray full of potted plants. 'All you've got to do is take each one out of the pot, together with all the soil, and then plant them in the garden. Be sure to water them straightaway.'

'Thanks, Mum,' said Charlie. 'That's great.'

'This is just the first tray. The garden centre manager overheard me telling the lady at the counter what they were for. When he heard about what you were doing he insisted on giving me a load more. He said they were not necessarily the most popular plants and they were unlikely to sell this season. So he said I could have them for free. You might want to get the others to help carry them through. There are four more trays.'

'Come on everybody, I need a hand,' said Charlie.

'While you're doing that I'll just pop my head inside and introduce myself to Mrs Elliot,' said Mother. 'Have you heard how Emma is?'

'No,' said Charlie.

'Poor thing,' said Mother. 'Right, I'll leave you to it. The car's unlocked.'

Charlie and the others went to the car, took out the trays of plants and carried them into the garden.

'This is so good,' said Penny. 'There's such a variety of plants. It will make a big difference to the garden.'

They soon finished digging the remainder of the garden. Knowing that they had lots of plants ready to go in made Charlie dig faster.

'Okay,' said Geraldine, 'we're ready to put the plants in. I'll place the pots where they should go. You then need to dig a hole slightly larger than each pot, remove the plants from the pot and plant them. Then we'll need to water them.'

While they were busy planting Geraldine's father turned up. After they had loaded all the bags of rubbish and weeds into the car, he had a look at the lawn.

'It's not as bad as I feared,' he said. 'I'll take out all the weeds, give it a quick trim using the shears and then plant some grass seed. I've brought some seeds that I had left over from when we reseeded part of our lawn at home. I'll use that. I'll trim the edges as well.'

'Well, I think that's about it,' said Mr Dewhurst. He had stood up and was admiring his work. She's as level as she'll ever be.'

'How bad was it?' asked Mr Primrose.

'Bad enough for a young lass to end up in the hospital,' said Mr Dewhurst. 'But it's safe enough now. Right, I must be going. Say cheerio to your auntie for me Penny. I'll see you later, son,' he said, as he ruffled Mickey's hair.

'See you, Dad,' said Mickey, who looked embarrassed.

'Right, let's get back to planting,' said Geraldine.

They carried on planting with Geraldine deciding the best position for the plants that needed lots of warmth and sunlight.

As they were getting towards the end, Geraldine's father called out, 'I've done all I can with the grass. It looks a bit more like a lawn now. Once the seed grows it will be fine. I'll leave you all too it.'

'Thank you, Father,' said Geraldine, as they all waved goodbye.

They continued planting until the final plant was in and watered.

'I think,' said Geraldine, 'we have done it.'

'I never ever want to plant another plant or weed another weed,' said Mickey.

'It wasn't that hard,' said Geraldine.

'You're being modest,' said Mickey. 'That gardening book is quite heavy.'

'We've all worked hard in our own way,' said Penny. 'It's just a shame Emma isn't here to see it. Come on, let's go to the patio and I'll get my auntie to come and look.'

They walked up to the patio. Mickey flopped into a chair and closed his eyes. 'Charlie,' he said, 'the next time you come across a book on gardening in the library, just hide it.'

Then Auntie Edith came out.

'What do you think, Auntie?' said Penny.

'I don't know what to say,' she said, as she took her handkerchief out and wiped away a tear. 'Look at all those plants and … this patio, you've repaired the patio!'

'It's the least I could do,' said Mickey.

'But if I'm not mistaken it was your father that did it,' said Auntie Edith, laughing.

'Well, I organized it. If I hadn't asked my dad it wouldn't have got done.'

'My mum got the plants,' said Charlie. 'And the garden centre manager let her have some for free.'

'Well, I never,' said Auntie Edith.

'And my dad has repaired your lawn,' said Geraldine. 'He's sown some seed so best not to go on it at the moment.'

'What I can say?' said Auntie Edith. 'Thank you from the bottom of my heart.'

'It was our pleasure,' said Penny.

'I think this calls for a celebration,' said Auntie Edith. 'You're too young for champagne but there's nothing to stop us from drinking homemade lemonade from champagne glasses. What do you say? Penny, come and give me a hand.'

They went into the house and came back out a minute later with Penny carrying a tray with five glasses.

'Help yourselves,' said Auntie Edith.

They each took a glass, including Penny who then held out the tray with the remaining glass for Auntie Edith. She was about to take the glass when they heard somebody walking down the side of the house.

'Hi everybody.'

They all turned round.

'Emma!' said Penny.

She was walking with crutches and her mother was following behind.

'How are you my dear?' said Auntie Edith.

'Not too bad,' said Emma.

'It's just a sprain,' said her mother. 'She's got to keep her weight off it and use crutches for the next week or so. But she insisted on coming here on the way home.'

'Well, you have come just in time to have a celebratory glass of lemonade,' said Auntie Edith. 'You make yourself comfortable on that chair,' she said as she took hold of the glass. When Emma had sat down Auntie Edith handed her the glass.

'The garden looks amazing,' said Emma. 'How did you manage to do all that?'

'I stayed focused,' said Mickey.

'Mickey!' said Penny and Geraldine together.

While they explained to Emma what had been going on, Charlie clutched his glass like a grown-up and surveyed the garden. With a little help they had done more than he had dared to hope. But as he admired their work he remembered his next challenge. That evening he was due to go to the climbing wall with his dad for another practice. In a week's time he would be taking part in the climbing competition. He took a large gulp of lemonade and wondered how he would ever manage to climb the dreaded overhang.

– CHAPTER 13 –

The dyno

Charlie moved easily up the wall, remembering the holds from last time. It was Saturday evening and he was in the sports hall of Heatherbridge High School. The climbing competition was just one week away. This would be his last opportunity to practise on the wall. He had to make this practice count.

'You're doing well,' said his father, from down below, as he paid out more rope.

But then Charlie got to the first sloper, shaped like a smooth boulder about the size of a rugby ball. This hold had defeated him last time.

'Remember what I taught you,' said his father.

Charlie tried to remember what he had said. But his father explaining it to him in the kitchen over a cup of tea was one thing. Actually doing it was another.

'Don't pull, Charlie,' Father shouted.

Charlie remembered his father had said this in the kitchen. The secret is to keep the arms straight and try to keep the bodyweight directly beneath the sloper. Charlie knew if he bent his arms and started to pull he would just slip off.

'You can do it, Charlie.'

But Charlie didn't yet know if he *could* do it. It was now or never. He put each hand in turn into his chalk bag behind him. Then he reached up with his right hand and made sure that as much of his hand as possible was touching the sloper. He knew that with more of his hand holding it the more friction and grip he would get.

'Straighten your arm, Charlie.'

'I am,' he said, as he straightened his arm.

Now it was time for the other hand. He swung his left arm up, keeping it straight even before it reached the sloper. As soon as his hand reached it he made sure his body stayed as close to the wall as possible. His hands seemed to be holding. Before he knew it he had left the sloper behind. He bit his lip and felt a surge of adrenaline. He had solved the problem of the sloper.

Charlie ascended steadily. The holds were tricky, including some slopers. But he was going well.

'Don't forget the quickdraw,' shouted Father.

Charlie looked up but could not see any nearby.

'It's by your knee,' said Father.

He looked down and felt annoyed with himself. He had forgotten about it in all the excitement of getting past the sloper. If he missed out a quickdraw during the competition he would be disqualified. He pushed the rope into the quickdraw and pressed on. Then he felt his head touch a hold. He had reached the overhang.

He put his rope into the next quick draw which was right by his head. He then half turned and half arched backwards, as he tried to assess the holds.

Charlie felt cramped up on the wall. This was new to him. Usually, everything felt open when climbing a wall indoors or a rock face outside. But now his way was blocked. The only way now was to move away from the vertical wall outwards along the roof of the overhang.

He knew that once he started he would not have long. While hanging upside down, the blood would be draining out of his arms and the lactic acid would soon build up, making his muscles ache.

'Go for it, Charlie,' shouted his father.

He bit his lip, took a deep breath and then set off. The good news was that the holds were easy. The bad news was that his arms soon began to ache. And as he moved away from the wall he certainly wasn't feeling cramped anymore. Instead, he felt terribly exposed, hanging high above the floor of the sports hall.

He kept going until he reached a big hold with which he could grip each side. Right next to it was a quickdraw. He pushed in the rope and this made him a lot safer. He allowed his feet to come off the overhang just to test the grip of the hold. He hung there for a moment. It was certainly a good hold. He swung back and forth and then managed to get his feet back onto the overhang. He still had several feet to go. But then he realized that he had what looked like an insurmountable problem.

There was one good looking hold right at the edge of the overhang. Either side of that, there was nothing. But that wasn't the problem. The problem was that between that hold and the hold he had reached there were no other holds. He managed to bring his feet a bit nearer his body. Then he stretched out with one of his hands and tried to reach the hold at the edge of the overhang. But he knew it was hopeless. It was way beyond his reach. He then tried hanging with one hand, his feet dangling below, and then reaching out with the other hand. He could stretch a few inches nearer but he was still a long way away. A grownup could reach it but there was no way he could. And then the aching in his muscles became just too much. He let go and ended up hanging a few feet below the overhang.

'I'll let you down, Charlie,' said Father.

Charlie slowly descended, shaking his arms to try to get the blood flowing and reduce the aches.

'I'll never reach that hold,' said Charlie, as his feet touched the ground. 'It's too far away.'

'You did well to reach that big two-handed hold on the overhang,' said Father. 'I'd be surprised if anybody else in your age group gets that far.'

'But what if they do?' asked Charlie.

'Well, if there's a tie for first place with two people reaching the same hold then the person who got there the fastest wins.'

'There must be a way of getting to that hold,' said Charlie, as he looked up again.

'It's impossible for somebody your age,' said Father. 'You're just not big enough. Although, having said that …' He stood looking up at the overhang, stroking his chin.

'Is there a way?' said Charlie.

'I don't know. It's a longshot. And you would only have one go. If it failed you would fall off and that would be the end of your go.'

'How could I reach it?' asked Charlie, who was getting impatient.

'A dyno,' said Father.

'A what?' said Charlie.

'A dyno. D-Y-N-O. That's when you jump from one hold to another.'

'But how could you jump while underneath an overhang?' asked Charlie.

'You could hang facing the wall like you did just now, swing back and forth as fast as you can and then let go so that you fly backwards. You might be able to reach the hold that way. Mind you, even if you reach it the chances of holding on are minimal.'

'It's a worth a try,' said Charlie.

'Okay, have a rest for a few minutes and give it a go,' said Father.

Ten minutes later Charlie was once more under the overhang. He reached the big handhold and pushed the rope into the quickdraw. He started to swing back and forth. Then he let go but he simply fell away from the overhang.

'You let go too soon,' shouted his father. 'Let go when you're swinging upwards more.'

He tried again. This time he stayed closer to the overhang but did not get near the edge.

Each time he tried and failed he would end up swinging on the rope. He then had to swing enough on the rope to reach the wall. He then had to climb back up the wall and under the overhang. He knew he could only do this one or two more times before he got too tired.

'Really go for it this time,' said Father.

Charlie swung back and forth and tried pushing against the overhang with his feet to give himself more speed. This time the dyno went much better. He was only a fingertip away from the hold at the edge of the overhang.

'Have you had enough?' asked Father.

'I'll try once more,' said Charlie.

This time, before he moved out under the overhang, he rested at the top of the wall. Then he climbed out to the two-handed hold. He swung back and forth, pushed off with his feet and let go at just the right moment. He craned upwards ready to grab the hold. But once more he was just a fingertip away.

'It's no good,' said Charlie when he got back down. 'There's no way I could do the jump any better than that last go.'

'I think you're right, Charlie,' said Father. 'Still, you gave it your best shot.'

The following week Charlie found it difficult to concentrate during school. He kept thinking about the overhang when he really should have been measuring angles on triangles, working out the total cost of an imaginary shopping list or remembering how to spell words in a spelling test.

But Saturday finally came. The climbing competition for his age group was due to start at 11 o'clock. He glanced at his watch as he sat in the back of the car. It was 10.15.

'Here we are,' said Father, as they pulled into the car park of Heatherbridge High School.

'Are you nervous Charlie?' asked Mother.

'A bit,' said Charlie.

Father parked the car, they got out and walked into the sports hall.

The hall was full of people. There were climbers of all ages doing stretching exercises and practising moves on the lower part of the wall. Some chairs had been set out along the side opposite the climbing wall. Charlie looked around for Mickey. He had said he might come. But Charlie couldn't see him.

'I'll go and sit down while you get Charlie registered,' said Mother.

'Okay,' said Father. 'Come on, Charlie, that's where we need to go.'

He was pointing towards a table at one end with a man sitting behind it with papers and clipboards. There was a queue of people in front of the table. They walked over and joined the queue. In front of them was a man with a boy that Charlie reckoned was about his age, although he didn't know him. The man turned round to look at them.

'Morning,' said Father.

'Morning,' said the man. 'Have you travelled far?'

'No, we live in Heatherbridge,' said Father. 'How about yourselves. Are you local?'

'No, we've come from Accrington.'

'Quite a journey,' said Father.

'When I heard about the competition I thought it would be an excellent opportunity for my son to get some recognition for his skills. I'm Lewis, by the way, Lewis Carruthers. This is my son, the eleven-year-old, soon-to-be twelve-year-old, Damon.'

'Pleased to meet you both,' said Father. 'I'm Martin Lupton. This is my son, Charlie.'

'Hi,' said Charlie.

'So are you a good climber, Damon?' said Father.

'Fairly good,' he said.

'He's being modest,' said Mr Carruthers. 'Looking at that wall, he should find it a piece of cake. Are you entering the competition, Charlie?'

'Yeah,' said Charlie.

'He'll be in the same age group as Damon,' said Father.

'Well, Charlie,' said Mr Carruthers, 'I'll apologize in advance as my son will probably steal the limelight. Still, it's the taking part that counts, isn't it? Well, unless you're a Carruthers, eh Damon?'

'Next please,' said the man behind the desk.

'Oh, I do apologize,' said Mr Carruthers. 'This is my son, the climber, Damon Carruthers.'

Father smiled and shook his head. Then it was Charlie's turn to register.

After he had signed in Charlie went over to the wall to warm up. He did a few stretches and practice moves. Then he heard a voice he recognized.

'Hi Charlie.' He turned round to see Mickey.

'Hi,' said Charlie.

'When are you on?' asked Mickey.

'Our competition starts at 11. It looks like there's about twenty of us. I don't know the order.'

Mickey looked up at the wall. 'Rather you than me, mate.'

'It's not too bad, but gets harder the higher you get,' said Charlie. Then Charlie looked across to the seats. 'Is that Emma?'

'Yep,' said Mickey, 'Unless she's got a twin sister who also walks on crutches. Geraldine's there too. They said they might come to watch you. No offence, but I think Geraldine's more interested in the school than watching you. Hey, what's going on over there?'

Charlie looked towards where Mickey was pointing. His father, Mr Carruthers and the man behind the table were having an animated conversation. Then Charlie's father walked over to them.

'Hello, Mickey,' said Father.

'Hello,' said Mickey.

'I'm afraid there's a problem, Charlie,' said Father. 'That Mr Carruthers has got wind of the fact that you have an artificial leg. He says you will have an unfair advantage. He wants you withdrawn.'

'But it's harder,' said Charlie, who felt himself welling up.

'I know but that's not what he thinks. He says your artificial leg can't get tired.'

'That's ridiculous,' said Charlie.

'Look, it will be fine,' said Father. 'They won't withdraw you.'

Then Mr Carruthers walked over to them. 'Listen, chaps, I've had a word with the organizers. It would be a bit rum for me to insist on you not taking part, young Charlie. So I've withdrawn my objection.'

'Thank you,' said Father, who sounded angry. 'That is very civil of you.'

'Not at all,' said Mr Carruthers. 'Mind you, if you do happen to win of course it will be rather overshadowed by the obvious use of an artificial aid.' Then he walked off.

'Just ignore him,' said Father.

Then the man who had been behind the table came over to the climbing wall. 'Will everybody taking part in the eleven and under competition please gather round. Right then, this is the order.'

Charlie wasn't listening. He just wanted to go home. In fact, he didn't even think his name was going to be read out. But then he heard his name. It was last on the list. The man then went through the rules but all Charlie heard was just noise. He wasn't really listening. He knew the rules anyway. You climb as high as you can without falling off. Finally, the man finished. Then he announced to the audience that the competition was about to begin and he read out the first name.

'Are you okay, Charlie?' said Father.

'Yeah, I'm fine.'

'Do you want to come and sit with Mum and me until it's your turn?'

'No, I'll wait over there,' he said, pointing to the corner near the door where the other climbers seemed to be.

'Okay,' said Father. 'Give that dyno all you've got. And forget about that Mr Carruthers.' He ruffled his hair and walked off.

Charlie went over to the corner. But deep down he had no intention of staying there. He kept going, walked through the door and sat down on the first chair he came to and started crying.

After a while, he heard the crowd groan and then clap. It didn't sound like the first climber had got very far. Not that he cared.

The minutes ticked by. Then the door opened. It was Mickey. He came over and sat by him. 'You alright mate? That Carruthers bloke was way out of order.'

Charlie wiped his eyes and said nothing.

'They've been useless so far by the way,' said Mickey. 'You'll be fine.'

'I'm not going to do it,' said Charlie.

'What do you mean you're not ...'

'What do you think I mean? You heard what that man said. Even if I win it won't mean anything.'

'Yeah, but that's only his opinion.'

'Maybe he's right,' said Charlie.

They sat in silence for a while.

Then Mickey said. 'Your accident was a real downer. If you didn't have an artificial leg there would be no problem.'

Charlie sat there staring down at the ground. Then he dried his eyes. 'That's it,' he said.

'What's it?' said Mickey.

'That's it,' said Charlie.

'You've lost me.'

'Mickey, I want you to go on a mission.'

'Mission is my middle name,' said Mickey. 'Uh, what do you want me to do?'

Charlie explained the mission to him.

'Uh, what do you need them for?' asked Mickey.

'Because I do. Will you do it?'

'Okay, but I hope you know what you are doing.' He got up and walked out.

Charlie sat for a moment and wondered what he was letting himself in for. He must be crazy, he thought. But he knew it was the only way. One thing was for sure, he knew that what he was about to try would be the ultimate challenge.

– CHAPTER 14 –

Beyond the rooftops

Charlie sat alone in the corridor outside the sports hall. He heard the name announced for the next climber. Shortly afterwards he heard loud groans from the audience followed by clapping. Somebody else had clearly not got very far up the wall.

He glanced at his watch. Not that the time mattered at the moment. But he wondered what was keeping Mickey. Would he be successful on his mission? Charlie thought he had better assume that Mickey would be successful. He started to make the necessary preparations. But if Mickey did not succeed then Charlie knew the preparations he was making would stop him from taking part in the competition.

Charlie had begun doing what he had to do when he stopped and sat motionless. The latest name to be called out was Damon Carruthers. If he was as good as his father had made out then the competition could soon be as good as over.

Charlie carried on with his preparation, but was listening all the time. There were one or two gasps, occasional clapping and every so often there were shouts of encouragement. But most importantly, the climb seemed to be still in progress. And the longer it went on the higher he must be getting.

Then Charlie thought he heard somebody shout 'ow'. It sounded like a lady. What was going on out there?

Then once more he heard people shouting encouragement.

Charlie finished his preparation and looked at his watch again. Where was Mickey?

The audience gave a loud groan then they clapped for what seemed like an age. Damon Carruthers had finished his go and it sounded like he had done well. But how far had he got? Had he climbed the overhang?

Then the door to the sports hall burst open. Mickey half fell into the corridor.

'Mission accomplished,' said Mickey, as he walked up to where Charlie was sitting, and handed him the crutches.

'What kept you?' said Charlie.

'I decided to go under deep cover.'

'What do you mean, *deep cover*?'

'I thought it would look suspicious if I just walked up to Emma, asked for her crutches, and then walked out again carrying them. So I decided to limp.'

'Limp?'

'Yeah. I made out I was injured so that I would look normal with the crutches.'

'Look normal? That would be a first. Anyway, what did Emma say? It's a wonder she didn't try and give you first aid.'

'I told her I was pretending and that you wanted to borrow her crutches.'

'Did she ask why?'

'Yeah. I told her what you were planning on doing. She said, "he'll never be able to do it".'

'Thanks for the encouragement,' said Charlie.

'It was her words not mine,' said Mickey. 'Mind you, I agree with her.'

'Thanks a lot,' said Charlie.

'Don't mention it,' said Mickey. 'By the way, be careful with those crutches. They're not easy to use.'

'I spent months walking with crutches,' said Charlie. 'I know what I'm doing.'

'Yeah, well, I'm just warning you. I think their tracking is off.'

'Tracking? They're crutches, Mickey. Crutches don't have tracking, let alone tracking that's off.'

'Try telling that to the wife of the mayor,' said Mickey. 'Although it was her fault for wearing fancy shoes. If she'd been wearing steel-capped boots, her toe wouldn't have felt anything when the crutch pressed down on it. Not that steel-capped boots would go with her flowery dress.'

'You trod on the toe of the wife of the mayor? That would explain the *ow* I heard.'

'I didn't tread on her toe,' said Mickey. 'It was the crutch.'

But then they heard the announcer speaking.

'And now everybody we come to our last competitor. As it stands, Damon Carruthers is winning. But please now give a round of applause for Charlie Lupton.'

Charlie stood up and put the crutches under his armpits.

'All the best, mate,' said Mickey. 'You can beat that Carruthers upstart.'

'Thanks,' said Charlie. 'By the way, how far did he get?'

'He got halfway under the roofy bit,' said Mickey. 'Then he dropped off.'

'You mean the overhang,' said Charlie.

'If you say so,' said Mickey.

'Get the door for me,' said Charlie, as he walked across the corridor.

Mickey held the door open.

Charlie got to the doorway. He glanced back at his artificial leg leaning against the chair. Then he took a deep breath, turned and walked into the sports hall.

The announcer was facing the audience and said, 'It does not seem that Charlie Lupton …'

But then Charlie saw somebody in the audience waving to the announcer and then pointing at Charlie.

The announcer turned around and looked at Charlie. At first, he seemed unsure what to do and stood motionless, still holding the microphone to his mouth. Then he lowered it, walked over to the audience and sat in a chair.

A hush had fallen over the sports hall. All that could be heard was the sound of the crutches banging on the floor.

Charlie glanced over to his mother and father sitting in the audience. He saw his father start to get up but then he sat back down as his mother put her hand on his arm.

When he reached the climbing wall the man doing the belaying handed him the rope. 'Are you going to be alright?' he asked.

'Yes,' said Charlie. 'I'll do the rope.'

'Okay, I'll check it when you're done.'

Charlie tied the rope to his climbing harness which he had put on in the corridor. When he had finished, the belayer started to check his knot and made sure the rope was threaded into the harness correctly. While he was doing this Charlie looked around. He saw Mr Carruthers leaning against a wall and staring down at the floor. Damon was sitting cross-legged on the floor in front of him. Then he saw Mickey limping over to where Emma and Geraldine were sitting. Geraldine shook her head and sighed as she watched Mickey. Then Charlie saw Emma giving himself a thumbs up.

'That's fine, Charlie,' said the belayer. 'The clock starts as soon as both feet are off the ground. I mean, well as soon as your foot leaves the ground. Sorry, Charlie.'

Charlie walked right up to the wall. He took his crutches out from under his armpits.

'I'll take those out the way.' He turned round to see the man who had been behind the table signing everybody in.

'Thanks,' said Charlie.

The man took them and walked off.

Charlie leant against the wall and looked up. With his artificial leg he could have climbed up the first part blindfolded. But now it was like starting a new climb for the very first time. He reached up and grabbed hold of two good handholds. Then he pulled on them and put his foot onto the first hold. He was now on his way. But he knew he was already off to a bad start. The secret of climbing is to only use the hands for balance as far as possible and use the legs to push up. But just to get off the floor he had already had to use up valuable arm strength.

Charlie knew there were two things he could essentially forget about from the outset. First, there was no way he would beat the time of Damon. He had to get further than him to win. Getting to the hold in the middle of the overhang would not be enough. Secondly, there was no point worrying about his climbing style. It would look ugly, and that was that.

Low down on the wall, there were plenty of holds and they were fairly close together. He was able to reach one on the right with his right leg. Thankfully his amputation had been below the knee. He hooked his knee around the hold. It felt safe enough. He had seen videos on the internet of amputees climbing without their artificial limbs. He knew it was possible to climb this way. But how long could he keep going?

He tried to use his good leg as much as he could to push upwards. But as the holds became fewer he found himself having to use his arms more and more. He got to one particular position where he had a good foothold for his left foot and a hold on his right where he could comfortably place his knee joint. A quickdraw was nearby and when he had pushed the rope in he rested for a while and shook his arms. They didn't feel too bad but once the lactic acid began to build up he knew it would then be only a matter of time before he could not go on any more.

As he felt the life coming back into his arms he leant back and looked out of the windows of the sports hall. He could see the rooftops of Heatherbridge and beyond them the mountains which surrounded the town. What was he doing on this wall when he could be out there in the mountains?

He heard somebody call out, 'Come on Charlie.'

He turned back to face the wall and looked up to see the slopers looming over him. But these no longer seemed the problem they once were. He chalked his hands well from the bag attached at the back of his harness. Then he set off and climbed through the first sloper easily. In fact, for some reason, it seemed a lot easier than before. But he did not have time to dwell on why. No sooner had he passed the first sloper he was then onto the next.

His muscles were now beginning to ache. Instead of his usual smooth climbing he now clambered and crawled up the wall. Then he came to the last quickdraw on the wall before the overhang. He pushed the rope in and swallowed hard as he sensed the claustrophobia of being tight up against the wall with the roof of the overhang only inches above.

He heard the people clapping but they may as well have not been there. They were far down below, like the village at the foot of the north face of the Eiger. They were just noise.

This was it. Every second delaying was a second wasted. He arched back, grabbed a hold on the overhang and began to move out. He had to use his arms even more without his artificial leg. He felt a sense of panic building up. The horribly exposed position and the race to get where he needed to get to before his arms gave out made him move fast, too fast. Gone were the precise and measured actions with which he usually climbed. Gone were the flowing moves as he went from one hold to the other.

He got to the good twohanded hold in the middle of the overhang panting for breath. He scrabbled with his left foot and right knee to try and get some grip. He had to take some strain off his arms and hands before he tried the next move. But it was impossible.

He had reached as far as Damon had got. There was no shame in failing now. It was now or never. His muscles were screaming to just get it over with. He gave up trying to get a grip with his legs. He pushed with his good leg against the overhang and started to swing. He was about to try a move he had tried several times before but which he had never succeeded in doing. Each time he had been a fingertip away from grabbing the hold at the edge of the overhang. Why should it be any different this time?

He desperately tried to get some speed up as he swung back and forth. As he looked down he saw the people below and for some reason, he focused on Mr Carruthers. He was looking up with a pitiful and disdainful smirk. This made Charlie momentarily feel angry but he knew he had to focus on getting the jump just right. He had to let go at precisely the right moment. But he had done that before, and it had not worked.

He decided he could manage two more swings then he would go for it. He looked ahead at the wall and saw a blur of the holds he had climbed up to get there. Including the slopers. The slopers, which had seemed so easier this time. Not only that, he sensed that somehow this jump might go better. But he could not work out why. Why should this jump be any different?

He was now on his final swing. Maybe it was no different. Maybe he was just imagining it. Perhaps he was getting fatigued. But then it came to him. He had barely time to even think about it. But in the moment before he let go, he knew what was different this time. A deep realization had dawned upon him. He knew why the slopers had been easier. He knew why this time he would surely succeed. He felt a surge of confidence and smiled a smile of grim determination and satisfaction. For as he let go and flew towards the handhold he was not encumbered with the weight of his artificial leg. This time he reached the handhold.

Now he was hanging on with desperation as the momentum from the jump threatened to loosen his grip. A quickdraw was right on the edge near the hold. He frantically reached down for the rope and tried to pull it up. But the rope felt tight. 'Slack,' he screamed, trying to make himself heard above the clapping and cheering. The belayer paid out more rope and he was able to push it into the quickdraw. Now all he had to do was to get properly onto the last vertical section.

He stretched out his left leg as far he could along the edge. He managed to get some sort of grip. Then he reached up blindly with his left hand. At first, there was nothing then he found a chunky hold. He wrapped his hand around it and pulled himself up. He now had his first proper view of the last few feet.

There were plenty of holds and above them all, was a big yellow hold with a piece of white tape next to it with the word 'Top' written on it. Three moves later and he was then able to grab the final hold with one hand. Then he reached up with the other hand. He hung there, fearful of letting go in case he had not convinced the judges that he had made it. But the noise from the crowd told him he had done it. He had completed the ultimate challenge.

He let go and began the slow descent to the floor as the belayer lowered him down.

He saw his father clapping and he thought he saw his mother wiping a tear from her eye. Mickey, Emma and Geraldine were cheering. Then he saw Mr Carruthers, sheepishly looking at the floor. But his son Damon was on his feet and clapping.

And as he continued to descend Charlie once more looked out of the windows beyond the rooftops, to the mountains where he knew he belonged.